Broken Star

Divided loyalties cause Fallon Vejar to leave his outlaw band when its leader decides to rob the bank in Vejar's home town. Despite having fled two years earlier after being accused of murder, his fears for Raya – the girl he left behind – make him return to Yancey.

Although he discovers that Raya is to marry his old friend Sheriff George Harker, Vejar is prepared to help Harker repel the very outlaws he'd abandoned. But Vejar's loyalties are again put to the test when the sheriff is shot and he is left to defend the hostile town on his own.

Now he must head towards a final showdown with all the odds against him.

Broken Star

Terry Murphy

A Black Horse Western

ROBERT HALE · LONDON

ISBN-10: 0-7090-7911-7
ISBN-13: 978-0-7090-7911-8

Robert Hale Limited
Clerkenwell House
Clerkenwell Green
London EC1R 0HT

Typeset by
Derek Doyle & Associates, Shaw Heath.
Printed and bound in Great Britain by
Antony Rowe Limited, Wiltshire

ONE

To be a hotel-keeper in Del Corsia, an untamed town close to the Mexican border, you needed a sixth-sense that detected trouble before it began. Frank Yarrow had the knack. Frank was not a fighting man, but a natural diplomat ready with the words that were known to calm the most savage breast. Though he could never think of himself as a hero, he modestly acknowledged that his ability to turn aside wrath had saved both lives and property in the past. Usually the property saved was his beloved Banner Hotel. Maybe it didn't rate as a hotel beside the classy places in the territory's larger towns, but the Banner was much appreciated by weary travellers and by local folk who enjoyed good food. The place meant everything to Frank, and there had been times when diplomacy wasn't enough and Frank had been forced to chance physical harm to preserve his little empire. So far he had been lucky.

But he had feared that his amazing good luck was about to desert him that evening, as he stood behind the mahogany desk in the hotel's dowdy foyer. From there he had an angled view of the busy dining-room. There were a few drummers in that evening, men with the gift of the gab, laughing too loud and too long while discussing the day's sales as they ate. Several staid ranchers who had business in town were treating their families to a meal served by two attractive and efficient Mexican waitresses. Then there were the regulars, the town's storekeepers and the like, the faithful who dined at the Banner every evening. But Frank was worried about a corner of the dining-room where sat six hard-faced men and a black-haired beauty who looked every bit as tough as her male companions. Though undoubtedly an outlaw gang, it wasn't a rowdy group of the type Frank had experience in handling. They weren't the sort who would take kindly to being preached at by a stranger, no matter how well intentioned that stranger might be. The men and the girl spoke little, and when they did it was in steady, subdued tones. But there were undercurrents, unseen and unheard, that the hotel-keeper was alarmed to pick up. If, as was likely, trouble erupted among these guests in his establishment, then Frank feared that neither he nor his hotel would survive.

Outlaws often passed through the town, spending enough to boost the economy of local trading places along the way. Rarely did they give any trouble, as Del Corsia had no bank and no other place worth robbing. But Frank suspected that there was some dangerous inner-gang dissent here that was close to tangible. When hard men such as these fell out it could turn real ugly.

Entering the dining-room, he used the pretence of clearing dirty crockery from tables to move nearer to the gang. His expert eye noted the worn handles on the low-slung six-shooters that all of the men were wearing. This told Frank that they were veteran gunslingers, proof that his apprehension was justified.

The totally relaxed, detached manner of one man who appeared to be superbly confident of his own reflexes and fighting ability, identified the leader for Frank. Shadows cast by the room's poor lighting accentuated a face that would have been strikingly handsome but for the imprint of a lifetime of degradation. Employing his uncanny skills, Frank pinpointed the source of potential trouble as an invisible animosity between the gang leader and a younger man with fair wavy hair that was worn long. In Frank's estimation the fair-haired outlaw, who was good-looking in a rugged kind of way, was as dangerous as the leader. The remaining four men were the common sort of desperadoes. Anonymous by their mediocrity, they neither added anything nor took anything away from what was between the two protagonists.

Frank heard the leader speak to the fair-haired man in a reasonable, conversational way. 'I don't see your problem, Fallon.'

This seemingly mild remark somehow charged the air with a tension that continued to build despite the interruption of a short burst of merriment from two young children sitting at a rancher's table. Frank noticed that the outlaw woman was worriedly studying first the leader and then the blond man.

'I can see what my problem is, which is all that matters to me,' the man named Fallon replied.

Though Fallon had answered in a moderate tone, Frank could detect a sharp edge to his words. This increased his fear, as it did the concern on the outlaw girl's lovely face. Frank made a mistake in moving to take a loaded tray of crockery from one of his waitresses in order to get closer to the gang. He heard the black-haired girl warn the leader sharply, 'Hold up on the talk, Ken.'

Turning his head to look steadily at Frank, the

gang leader gave him a white-toothed smile. But that couldn't disguise the menace in his voice when he said, 'Best get yourself back out in the foyer, *mi amigo*. Looks as how there's a couple of *hombres* wanting to check in.'

A quick glance told Frank that the foyer was empty, but he wasn't about to argue. He was aware of the man named Fallon moving slightly in his seat to position his holstered .45 clear of the table. There was going to be trouble for sure, big trouble, but now Frank could do nothing to avert it. He could actually feel the short hairs rise on his forearms, and an icy-cold prickle ran down his spine. Rare though they were, it was situations like this that took the pleasure out of running a business in Del Corsia.

Behind his desk once more, Frank Yarrow risked a sideways glance into the dining-room. Though the gang remained quiet, the atmosphere was more fraught than ever. The other diners were oblivious to the fast-mounting tension, but it was causing Frank extreme anxiety. One time when the James boys had spent two nights at his hotel, his nerves had been continuously on edge. With a strict Jesse in control, that occasion had passed without incident. But now there was dread in his veins, toxic and deadening.

He gave an involuntary jerk, upsetting the

inkpot as he saw the fair-haired outlaw shift his chair back a little from the table. Dabbing at the spilled ink with a blotter, Frank feared that whatever it was between the two men had come to a head. The young outlaw got suddenly to his feet. Violence in the extreme was about to explode. Not realizing that he had been holding his breath, a relieved Frank released it in a snort when the fair-haired man didn't go for his gun. He and the gang leader seemed to be conversing. That was a good sign.

'You walk away from this table, Vejar, and you'd better turn and slap leather before you get to that door.'

Fallon Vejar knew that this was no idle threat. Their harsh way of life didn't embrace consideration for others. Ken Klugg would not let danger to the other people in the dining-room, including children, deter him from gunplay. Yet Vejar also knew that he had no choice but to leave. It was ironic that he wouldn't be welcome in his hometown of Yancey, yet it was to save that town that made it necessary for him to split with the Klugg gang after two financially rewarding years.

He said quietly. 'You leave me with no option but to go, Ken. There are people back in Yancey who I care about.'

'There are people you should care about right here at this table,' Klugg retorted.

'You are right, there are,' Vejar conceded. 'But you are pushing me to choose between them and the folks back home.'

'There should be no choice to make after what we've been through together,' Klugg argued.

'This is silly,' Gloria Malone put in nervously, using a hand to brush back a sweep of blue/black hair from her face. Her foolishness in speaking up worried Vejar. It didn't pay to talk back to Ken Klugg, particularly as she was obviously taking Vejar's side. Klugg had for some time been seething with envy over the relationship that had developed between Gloria and Vejar.

Gloria had been with them for ten months, since she had unknowingly jeopardized a bank job in New Mexico. Down on her luck, Gloria had alerted the law in town by bungling her single-handed hold-up attempt on a merchandise store, just as the Klugg outlaw band was about to hit the bank. With its renowned audacity, the gang had plundered the bank and then rescued Gloria, who soon became a valuable member of the outlaw band. She was good with a handgun and a brilliant shot with a rifle. Wherever the gang went, the sultry, dark-skinned, smouldering-eyed Gloria held just about every man under her spell. But no man, no matter how drunk, dared to make a move towards her.

'Stay out of this, Gloria,' Klugg warned in a half whisper.

'No, I won't,' Gloria said stubbornly. The brightness of her eyes owed nothing to fear. That was an emotion with which Vejar doubted Gloria had ever been acquainted. 'You can't afford to lose your second in command, Ken. You and Fallon work well together. It doesn't have to be Yancey. There are other towns, other banks.'

'I give the orders,' Klugg told her flatly. 'I say we'll hit the bank and Yancey, so Yancey it is.'

'This time I'm going to have my say, Ken,' Vejar argued.

'There can be only one leader, Fallon,' Klugg stated coldly, 'and that's me.'

'Then count me out,' Vejar said, getting to his feet.

That was a rash statement for someone with nowhere to go to make. Vejar was keenly aware of that. Having left his hometown under a cloud two years ago, trying to return would probably be unwise. Since joining Klugg he had become moderately wealthy robbing trains, stage-coaches, and banks. But he had become a big spender used to living it up, and what money he had put by wouldn't last long. The forces of law and order were becoming more effective these days, and a lone outlaw had little hope of making a living, or even of carrying on living.

'Sit down, Fallon,' Gloria pleaded. 'He'll kill you.'

Dismissing this with a shake of his head, Vejar kept his gaze steadily on Klugg. 'I'm walking out of here right now. You know that I've always shaded you, Ken, so don't risk it.'

'Maybe you do have the edge on me, Fallon, maybe you don't,' Klugg said, the hint of a grin twitching at the corners of his mouth. 'But remember, you will be walking away, with your back to me.'

Vejar needed no reminder that he was putting himself at a disadvantage. But he had complete faith in his gunfighting skill. That skill had forced him to leave Yancey and had then brought him infamy as a member of the Klugg outlaw bunch. He was sure that he would know if Klugg went for his gun, and he could turn and fire before the leader of the gang's six-gun had cleared its holster. Yet he hoped that wouldn't happen. Though they differed in many ways, he had no quarrel with Ken Klugg. Respecting each other, they had come as close to being friends as was possible in the kind of life they led. The two of them had watched over each other through the years.

Without speaking another word, Vejar turned. As he took his first slow pace in the direction of the door, he heard Gloria Malone cry out, begging him not to go. Unheeding, he took one more step, then another. It had gone very quiet in the dining-room as everyone there but the children sensed that they were caught up in a serious situation. Doubting that Klugg could stand the loss of face at having someone walk out on him, Vejar kept on going slowly towards the door.

Ken Klugg was a man of honour, although many who knew him would say that it was a perverted sense of honour. Even so, Vejar accepted that the gang leader wouldn't shoot him in the back without warning. Klugg would call his name just before going for his gun. But that had not happened, and now Vejar had reached the dining-room door. A few feet ahead of him the visibly trembling hotel-keeper stood in the foyer, and still Klugg hadn't made his move. Then, with Vejar framed in the doorway, Klugg shouted.

'Vejar.'

Moving fast, every nerve and muscle co-ordinating perfectly. Vejar drew his gun and turned, dropping into a crouch, in one fluid movement. Women screamed and men were frantically pulling children towards what they hoped was safety. Vejar, as immobile as a statue in his crouching stance, was bemused. Relaxed in his chair, thumbs of both hands hooked in his belt, Ken Klugg had made no attempt to draw his gun. He had played a suicidal game, relying solely on the total control that Vejar had over himself.

Straightening up, Vejar let his gun slide back into its holster. An inaudible, concerted sigh of relief filled the room. Leaning one shoulder against the doorframe, Vejar waited. Staying silent for some minutes, Klugg sought Vejar's gaze and held it.

Then, speaking evenly, Klugg said, 'This is neither the time nor the place, Vejar. But if you leave now, the next time we come face to face only one of us will walk away.'

With a nod to signify that he understood, Vejar replied, 'I wouldn't want that.'

'Neither would I, Fallon, but it's your call.'

Gloria was looking at Vejar; her dark eyes were trying to convey a message to him. But Vejar couldn't read it. Maybe he didn't want to read it. The girl had come to mean a lot to him. Probably too much. For some time he had been alarmed at the fast rate he had been surrendering a God-given freedom to their relationship. He turned on his heel and walked out into the foyer. As he passed him the hotel-keeper mumbled, 'Thank you.' Unable to grasp why the man would want to express gratitude to him, Vejar walked on without replying.

Out on a street, Vejar looked at the skyline over the hills beyond the town. The sun had dropped out of sight some time ago, but it had left a memory of gold where it had set. He paused for a moment to take a long, deep breath. This was one of those times in life when the trail ahead forked, and you knew that nothing would ever be the same again whether you took the left or the right fork. After a few minutes' reflection, he walked off towards the livery where he had left his horse. Habit had him keep to the shadows as he went.

Vejar was aware that when he reached the livery and saddled up he had a mighty decision to make. He had to make a choice of loyalties. Did he owe it to the people who were once his friends back in Yancey to warn them that the Klugg outlaw band would soon hit their town? Did that take precedence over betraying Klugg, Gloria, and the others, with whom he had lived with for so long, sharing many perils, so often facing sudden death?

Either choice would be the wrong one, Vejar accepted unhappily. It seemed to him that by walking just one hundred yards from the Banner

Hotel he had come to another world, a world considerably less secure than the one he had just left.

TWO

He kept his horse climbing, reining into the shadows of some pines from where he saw the last ray of sunlight snatched over the horizon. The sun had gone and long shafts of sullen light poured through the still silhouettes of distant ranches and rolling hills. Immediately below him, ghostly in a low-lying mist, was the town of Yancey. Stopping his horse, Fallon Vejar sat unmoving in the saddle, looking down, wondering why a homecoming should touch a man's spine with an icy finger. He was gripped in a state of indecision by the realization that it would be easier to ride off over and beyond the distant hills than it would be to cover the last quarter of a mile into town.

Raya's soft voice came out of the darkness, playing back to him the words she had spoken so pensively two long years ago. 'I don't want you to leave, of course, Fallon. But you must go for your own safety. Whether you come back one day, or send for me to join you, I will be waiting. If needs be I will wait forever.'

Vejar had not sent for her, neither had he come back. Until now. But it wasn't as a hero, the town's favourite son returning after having atoned for the sins that he was believed to have committed; the reputation he had gained since riding away from Yancey had, now, probably alienated those in the town who once considered that he had been done an injustice.

Yet he could not abandon the good folk who were once his friends to the merciless Klugg gang. But by going against Ken Klugg he would be putting Gloria at risk, and that thought tormented him. Even so, he rediscovered the resolve that had ebbed in him since leaving Del Corsia. Letting out a long, slow breath, as if a tightly coiled spring inside him had relaxed a bit, Vejar started his horse down the slope to enter the east end of Yancey.

The lights of the Hero of Alamo saloon parted a thickening dusk to become a guiding beacon. He passed what was Ma Cousins' boarding-house when he had left town, but was now dilapidated. The windows were no longer glazed. They were the unseeing eyes of the past.

Dismounting and hitching his horse at the rail, he hesitated for a brief moment outside the door of the saloon before going in. Yancey's largest saloon afforded every facility for fools, young and old, to part with their money. It was busy now with groups of noisy cowboys starting out on an evening of dissipation. The far end of the long room was dotted with round tables at which sat gamblers and solid businessmen. Circling among them were gaily plumaged ladies wearing expensive dresses and jewels that glittered in the artificial lighting whenever they moved. They were rich in material possessions but poor in chastity. The town had thrived and expanded fast in Vejar's absence.

The heads of people he had once known turned to see who had entered. If they remembered him, then they were careful not to show it before looking away. At the bar, he ordered whiskey from a bartender who was a stranger to him. A pretty girl clad in insufficient clothing, thin and broken shoes, and a faded shawl, came up to lean nonchalantly against the bar at his side. A scarlet, practised smile was draped across her face. Aged no more than seventeen, the girl deftly rolled a cigarette while awaiting a response from him.

Ignoring the girl, Vejar put one foot on the brass rail as he used the huge mirror behind the bar to study the seated drinkers in the bar. Mentally putting names to faces that seemed farther distant than two years, he tensed ready for action when a figure came up close behind him. At the same time a sudden fear had the girl at his side move quickly away.

Then Vejar relaxed on recognizing his old friend George Harker. Though a hard man, the sophisticated Harker had impeccable poise that put him on terms of intimacy with top people in all quarters of Yancey. With a lithe and gracefully formed physique, he was resplendent in an olive-green jacket and darker green cravat complementing a high-collared shirt. Incredibly handsome despite many a bruising fight in his wild days, he smiled a welcome at Vejar.

'George,' Vejar said, making a quarter turn, one elbow remaining on the bar as he pointed with the forefinger of his other hand at the silver star pinned to his friend's chest. 'I heard that they made you sheriff.'

'I've been hearing about you, too, Fallon,' Harker replied meaningfully. 'The price on your head goes up every month.'

'You figuring on collecting the reward, George?'

Harker shook his head. For all his impressive fighting record, he was a placid man unless he was roused, and he didn't rouse easily. 'Nope. We have been buddies too long for me to even consider it, Fallon. I'm not looking for extra bother. It takes me all my time to keep a grip on this town.'

'Yancey sure has grown up since I rode out, George,' Vejar remarked, looking around at the bustling saloon trade. He wanted to ask about Raya, but first needed to discover how the town might react to his return.

'Some things haven't changed,' the sheriff told him in a cautionary tone. He used a nod of his head to indicate a vacant chair backed against a wall. 'When you came in, Jack Smiley was sitting right there.'

'So?' Vejar questioned with a shrug of indifference. A former grub-line rider, Smiley did menial work for the Poole brothers.

'He isn't there now,' Harker replied pointedly.

'You're saying that he's riding out to tell the Poole brothers that I'm back in town, George?'

'I'd wager my tin badge on it.'

'But I killed Billy Poole in a fair fight,' Vejar protested.

'I believe you,' Harker confirmed, nodding gravely, 'but the Pooles don't, and you don't have one witness. Lew, Michael and Ben aren't the forgetting and forgiving kind, Fallon.'

'Are you telling me to get out of town before the Pooles come riding in, hell-bent on making trouble, George?'

'Unless I'm greatly mistaken, that is what will

happen, Fallon,' Harker answered cautiously. 'The Poole brothers own the biggest ranch in the territory. They have a lot of power hereabouts, and nobody's going to complain if they gun you down.'

'Let them try, George,' Vejar said. 'I'll be ready for them.'

Keeping his glistening black eyes on Vejar, Harker explained in a flat tone, 'I know that, Fallon. But let me tell you how it is. I'm proud to be wearing this star, and I won't betray the people who placed trust in me by making me sheriff. If you being back here means there'll be gunplay, then I have to warn that I won't treat you any different than anyone else.'

'I wouldn't expect you to, George,' Vejar conceded. 'But giving the Pooles a chance to settle an old score isn't what brought me back here.' He accepted a cigar and a light from Harker before going on. 'Yancey is a right prosperous town now, and that hasn't gone unnoticed.'

Harker's face became cold and calculating. His teeth clamped hard on the lighted cigar they were holding. 'Are you saying what I think you're saying, *compadre*?'

Vejar nodded.

'The bank, Fallon?'

Again Vejar nodded.

'Come on,' an interested Harker said, beckoning one of the bartenders. 'I'll get us a bottle and we'll find a table.'

When they were seated and Harker was pouring each of them a drink, Vejar remarked, 'I intended to book in at Ma Cousins' place, George, but I see that it's just a ruin now.'

Harker nodded. 'Ma caught some kind of fever a year or so ago, and died real fast. But you can bed down in a cell at the jailhouse. That's no problem, Fallon.'

'You're a true buddy, George,' Vejar said, raising his glass, 'and I'll drink to that.'

With his glass still on the table, Harker advised, 'Hold on there for a minute before you raise your glass to me, Fallon. Just so's there won't be any misunderstanding between us later, I should tell you that me and Raya are together now.'

Harker's words made Vejar reel inwardly in shock. Though his resolve to warn the sheriff about the Klugg gang had just taken a battering, loyalty to an old friend would ensure that he did so. Yet what modicum of pleasure he had felt at coming home had died a sudden and painful death. He eyed the sheriff silently and coldly as he raised his glass to his lips, still unspeaking.

*

'You certain sure that it's Vejar you saw?' Lew Poole asked.

Lew, the eldest of the three surviving Poole brothers, was a stocky, muscular man standing five feet six inches in height, with a rugged countenance that reflected his callous disposition. A man with a cruel and cunning nature, Lew Poole was not nearly as tough as his reputation proclaimed. But Jack Smiley was not the stuff of which heroes are made, and he cringed when questioned by Lew.

'It was him, Lew,' Smiley whined. 'It was Fallon Vejar, sure as shootin'.'

'What's this about Vejar?'

Having just come into the Twin Circle ranch house, Michael Poole dismissed Smiley with a contemptuous glance, and snapped the question at his brother.

'Vejar's back in town. Sitting drinking in The Hero,' Lew answered.

'He won't be sitting there for much longer.' A thin man with the sly face of a coyote, complete with slanted eyes in which cunning gleamed bright, Michael unbuttoned his coat, took it off and threw it on to a chair. 'Young Billy will never be at rest until we deal with the man who murdered him in cold blood.'

'Steady now, Michael,' Lew warned, as he saw the conflict in his brother's face, the sudden flare of his focused eyes, the tightening jaw muscles that widened his mouth. 'I'm as riled as you that this varmint's come back, but it ain't wise to go riding off into town half-cocked.'

'There's only one of Vejar, and there's three of us, Lew.'

'Four,' Jack Smiley said, tentatively.

With a flick of his thumb, Lew Poole sent a coin spinning through the air and Smiley deftly caught it.

'Get out of here, Smiley,' Lew ordered brusquely. As Smiley obeyed, Lew turned to Michael. 'Where's Brother Ben?'

'He's got some of the hands fixing that broken rail down at the corral.'

'Go get him,' Lew said. 'The three of us need to discuss this. We got to do something real quick about Vejar, but we got to let George Harker see us do it right, Michael.'

An excellent choir was singing a hymn when Mary Alcott reached the lower end of Yancey's main street. The sound seemed to escape from the church to float through the air unattached and eerie. Mary hesitated outside, reluctant to enter and impart news that she knew would upset her dearest friend. Plucking up courage, she reached for the door handle. The latch made an unexpectedly loud clank as Mary lifted

it, making her both embarrassed and uncomfortable. But the singing continued uninter-
rupted as she tiptoed inside and noiselessly
closed the door.

Reverend Thomas Hailey, a small man with an
abundance of grey hair, conducted a choir made
up of young women. With a pulpit for a rostrum,
the choirmaster's head jerked this way and that,
pausing in a listening position occasionally, first
to the left and then to the right, then nodding
contentedly. Then the combined voices faded
into a pregnant silence that was invaded by a
solo female voice. Both hands raised, head
thrown back, the Reverend Halley coaxed out a
truly wonderful voice that sang 'Jerusalem.'

The singer was Raya Kennedy, Mary's best
friend. Angelic in the church setting, Raya had
long, straight golden hair framing a schoolgirl's
face that had a look of sadness. Her slender
build added to the pre-puberty illusion.
Forgetting her mission for a moment, Mary
stood quietly, enthralled by the beauty of the
voice that fully complemented the inspiring
hymn. When the singing ended, Raya's exquisite
voice seemed to live on as a pleasing echo.

With difficulty, Mary brought herself back to
the task that had brought her to the church. She
hurried up the aisle to a surprised Raya.

'Mary, what brings you here?' Raya enquired,

curiosity creasing her brow.

Up closer, the illusion of a slim, honey-haired child faded. Raya the girl-child looked older and tireder. Orphaned at the age of five, she had lived a harsh life until Mary had befriended her. Now living with Mary and her parents, she had become part of the family. Raya was also a partner with Mary in a small dressmaking business. Yet she hadn't shed the sensitive skin of someone who has experienced how cruel and heartless people could be.

'Can we talk for a moment, Raya?' Mary asked, more a ploy to broach a difficult subject than it was a question.

'Of course.'

As the choir began rehearsing another hymn, Raya led the way to an alcove. When she turned with her back to the wall she was holding herself tight, stiff. Her grey eyes returned Mary's gaze anxiously. Like all those who had suffered badly in life, Raya lived in constant expectation of more hard knocks.

'What is it, Mary? What's happened?'

Taking hold of both of her friend's hands. Mary spoke gently. 'I thought that I ought to tell you, Raya. Fallon Vejar is back in town.'

There was a prolonged silence. Then Raya uttered a bemused, 'Why?' Aware that the one-word question wasn't directed at her, Mary made no attempt to reply. The choir was singing 'Were You There When They Crucified Our Lord', and Mary had to lean close to catch Raya's words as she spoke again.

'This is the last thing I wanted to happen, Mary. It will spoil everything.'

'Not necessarily,' Mary tried to assure her. 'You are with George now. It could be that Fallon is just passing through, and he'll be gone by morning.'

'No.' Raya shook her head almost violently. 'The very fact that Fallon has come back means trouble, Mary.'

That was something that Mary couldn't argue against, so she remained quiet. She wished that everything could revert to what it had been an hour ago, clean and fresh and eternal. But it couldn't and it wouldn't, because Fallon Vejar had ridden back into town.

They left the saloon together to walk slowly down the dark street. Though Vejar was of a somewhat taciturn nature, they conversed in the way of reunited old friends who have much to catch up on. But George Harker sensed that his long-term friendship with Vejar had been fractured earlier by mention of his relationship with Raya Kennedy. Raya and Vejar were to have been married when Vejar's gunfighting had parted them. Harker balanced out the guilt he felt with the thought that Vejar had abandoned Raya. He guessed that the rift between Vejar and him would eventually close, but doubted whether it would ever again be quite the same between them.

Vejar went quiet as they passed the feed store. Harker accepted that his friend was reliving a bad memory. It was from an alleyway just across the street that Billy Poole, who had lost heavily to Vejar in a game of poker that long ago evening, had taken a shot at Vejar. It was a mistake to pull a gun on a gunfighter of Fallon Vejar's calibre, and an even bigger mistake to miss. Vejar had drawn and released a shot at where he had seen the flash of Billy's gun. The sound of gunfire had brought people out on the street. Billy Poole had been found dead in the alley, his spine shattered by a bullet. It had been plain to Harker and some others that Billy had turned to flee after shooting at Vejar. But the three surviving Poole brothers had played on the fact that Billy had been shot in the back. His reputation as a fast gun and a man who seemed to attract trouble, had gone against Vejar, who fled before Rory Kelvin, the then sheriff who was under pressure from the town's hierarchy, could arrest him for the murder of Billy Poole.

Harker broke the silence as they walked, by

asking, 'How many are there in the Klugg gang, Fallon?'

'Klugg and five others since I left,' Vejar replied.

'Is Klugg someone to be reckoned with?'

'He's the best, George.'

Staying silent, Harker put out a hand to halt Vejar, who had himself noticed a subtle change in the shadows cast by a building ahead of them. Someone standing close to the building had moved slightly. This was Harker's town, so Vejar stayed put while the sheriff kept in tight to the buildings beside them as he moved swiftly and noiselessly on. Hearing an animal-like squeal, Vejar saw the figure of a man ejected from the shadows. From the way the figure was hurtled across the sidewalk to crash face down in the dusty street, Vejar assumed that the unfortunate man had been propelled by a kick from Harker.

'Just a drunk,' Harker told Vejar, when he joined him down the street.

The man lay unmoving in the street, either unconscious from alcohol or rough treatment from Harker. Vejar remarked, 'You're as alert as ever, George. No one will ever get the drop on you.'

'Don't tell me that you didn't notice something up ahead of us, Fallon.'

Not answering this, Vejar asked a question,

'How many deputies you got?'

'One,' Harker answered ruefully. 'And that's old Dan Matthews.'

'That's as good as being on your own,' Vejar commented solemnly, 'You'll need some good men backing you when you go against Ken Klugg, George.'

With a shrug, Harker said, 'I won't find them in Yancey. Everyone here these days is bent on making money, not getting themselves shot.'

'So you will have to rely on yourself,' Vejar mused. 'You've got the speed and the skill. You're good, George.'

'Perhaps not as good as you.'

'That's not what I was leading up to,' Vejar explained. 'What I'm saying is that even the best of gunslingers can't take on the Klugg outlaw band alone.'

'Maybe the two of us could,' Harker suggested tentatively.

'It's not that easy for me, George.'

'Loyalty to your old gang?'

'Not exactly,' Vejar replied. 'I made it pretty plain to Ken Klugg that I'll act against him if he hits the bank here at Yancey.'

Puzzled by this, Harker enquired, 'I've never known you to duck a fight, Fallon, so what's the problem?'

'It's not straightforward.'

Though he had observed Vejar's adverse reaction to learning that Raya and he were going out together, Harker hadn't thought for one moment that it would come to this. He chose his words carefully. 'Is it something between us, Fallon?'

'No, it has nothing to do with you or anyone else here in Yancey,' Vejar replied.

They had reached the jailhouse, and an even more mystified Harker unlocked the door. Changing the conversation, he said, 'You have the place to yourself, Fallon.' He waved a hand towards the cells. 'Feel free to choose the best bed in the house.'

'Thanks,' Vejar said.

'I'll look you up in the morning,' Harker told him, pausing at the door to speak over his shoulder to Vejar. 'I heard tell that there's a girl riding with the Klugg outfit.'

The sheriff meant this to be taken as a question. But Vejar ignored it completely. Certain that he had touched on what was bothering his friend, Harker said no more. Holding the door open for a moment, he gave Vejar the chance to say something. When his friend uttered not one word. Harker stepped out into the night and closed the door behind him.

THREE

It was ten o'clock in the morning and trading on Yancey's main street was already brisk when Raya Kennedy walked to the bank. She had gone quickly, not wanting to encounter Fallon Vejar on the street. Now, with two other customers between her and the teller, she kept watch through the bank's open door. Why was she doing that? Raya didn't know the answer. Perhaps it was because if she saw him coming in her direction she could escape him. Or maybe it was that she secretly wanted to at least catch a glimpse of Fallon. That was understandable, as they had once planned to marry, but inexcusable because she was now George Harker's girl. George was a gentleman who was highly respected by everyone in town, whereas after being forced out of Yancey, Fallon had become an outlaw with a price on his head.

Raya gave an involuntary little jump as a

shadow fell across the doorway. The possibility that it was Fallon Vejar both unnerved and thrilled her a little. But it was a woman who entered. Around the same age as Raya, she was dark-complexioned; her black hair, worn long, was pulled back and tied with a single ribbon. She wore a crimson shirt and had a pair of saddle-bags draped over her left shoulder. Pausing to look curiously around her, the way strangers do on arriving, she flashed a brilliant smile at Raya.

'So, this is Yancey,' the woman said, speaking as though she and Raya had just ridden into town together.

Taken aback by this direct approach, Raya's natural shyness overwhelmed her. All she could manage to say was, 'Good morning.'

'Are you from around these parts?' the dark woman asked. 'I'm so glad to see a friendly face. I always feel so out of it, so alone, on arriving at somewhere new to me.'

Smiling sympathetically, Raya nodded. 'Yes, I have lived here all my life.'

'Then we could be neighbours soon.'

'That would be nice,' Raya responded, having swiftly come to like her new acquaintance.

'Forgive me,' the woman said, with a self-deprecating little smile. She put out her hand, hesitating slightly as she introduced herself.

'Carmel Morrow.'

'Raya Kennedy,' Raya said, as she shook the woman's hand. 'You are considering moving to Yancey?'

'If I can find the right place. My brother and I have worked hard all our lives making money for others, and now we want to go into ranching ourselves. Nothing big, nothing difficult to handle. Just something interesting and rewarding.'

'I understand,' Raya said, with a sympathetic smile. 'I do hope that you find what you are looking for.'

'So do I,' Carmel Morrow said wistfully. She hooked a thumb under the strap joining the saddle-bags and took them from her shoulder. 'First things first, though. I need to become a solid citizen by opening an account here.' A sudden thought clouded her face and she enquired, 'I hope I'm not risking our savings. Is Yancey a safe town, Raya?'

'Absolutely,' Raya assured her, giving an embarrassed little giggle before adding, 'Mind you, I'm biased, as I'm going to marry the sheriff next spring.'

'You can't get safer than that,' Carmel laughed.

'That's very true,' Raya agreed proudly. 'There's nobody within two hundred miles of

Yancey who would dare to go against Sheriff George Harker.'

Giving Raya's arm a little squeeze, Carmel said, 'That's very reassuring. Thank you, Raya. Maybe I'll get an invite to the wedding if we settle here.'

'You most certainly will, Carmel, both you and your brother.'

'That's nice of you.' The teller's position was now vacant and Carmel gave Raya a gentle nudge with her elbow. 'There you go.'

Having seen Raya go into the bank, Fallon Vejar pretended to study the items in a gunsmith's window while keeping an eye on the bank doorway. The street was a peaceful scene of people going about their legitimate business. It pained him to imagine how drastically that would change when Ken Klugg and his gang arrived. Since venturing out that morning, he had met several folk he had once known well, but who now passed him by without speaking. This made him wonder how Raya would react to his return. During a largely sleepless night in the jailhouse, he had done some deep thinking. He had reasoned that as he was sure to meet Raya at some time, then the sooner he did so the better. Though he still had strong feelings for Raya, his days as an outlaw had forever separated him from her. Though it would be painful for him, he had to let her go. The air between Raya, Harker, and him had to be cleared if he was going to work with the sheriff.

Raya reappeared, coming out of the bank and turning down the street without even a glance in his direction. Vejar started after her, but stopped again as a rider he recognized as Ben, the youngest of the Poole brothers, came slowly down the street. Passing Raya, Ben Poole headed unhurriedly towards Vejar. Anticipating trouble from the renowned brawler, Vejar stood on the edge of the sidewalk, waiting.

Ben Poole was a big man, whose size and strength was feared greatly. He reined up in front of Vejar; a holstered Colt .45 resting on a right thigh that was as thick as a tree trunk. Vejar was confident that there would be no gunplay. The heavily muscled Ben's movements were far too slow for him to draw on Vejar. In the way of all bullies, Ben Poole never started a fight that he wasn't certain he could win. But a cautious Vejar quickly scanned all of the doorways and side alleys in the vicinity, suspecting that the other two Poole brothers might be lying in ambush. But the area was clear.

Then, out of the corner of his eye, he saw a woman exit the bank. There was something immediately familiar about her. With two saddle-bags slung over her shoulder, she turned and walked off away from him. Though he hadn't seen her face, the way she held herself and her walk half convinced him that it was Gloria Malone. Vejar accepted that all that kept him from being fully convinced of the woman's identity, was his fervent hope that it wasn't Gloria.

Seeing the black-haired outlaw girl in Yancey was deeply disturbing for Vejar. Ken Klugg was moving in on the town more rapidly than Vejar had expected. The immediate threat that was Ben Poole instantly became a secondary, unimportant issue. Vejar had to force himself to bring his attention back to the thuggish Ben.

With both hands resting on his saddle horn, Poole's dark eyes had within them a permanent glint of amusement as though he was laughing at himself. There was a deceptive aura of childish innocence about the big man. This no longer fooled anyone who had seen his massive fists beat opponents to a pulp, or his murderous intent when wielding the long-bladed knife that he habitually carried.

Annoyed at having missed an opportunity to speak with Raya, and perplexed by seeing Gloria in town, Vejar tersely enquired, 'Have you got something you want to say, Poole?'

Not replying, Ben Poole sat staring at Vejar for several minutes, his large, flat face expressionless. Then he slowly raised his right hand and pointed the forefinger at Vejar. After a minute or so had passed, Poole lowered the hand, pulled the head of his horse round, and rode off up the street, keeping his mount at a walking pace.

Aware that what had just happened was simply the start of what would inevitably occur between the Poole brothers and him, Vejar stood for a moment watching the broad back of the departing Ben Poole. Then he pulled down his Stetson to shield his eyes from the sun as he made his way to the sheriff's office.

Finding George Harker sitting behind his desk engaged in some paperwork, Vejar explained who Gloria Malone was, and how he had seen her leaving Yancey's bank.

'Getting the lie of the land?' Harker asked, raising one eyebrow questioningly. 'You say that she was carrying a saddle-bag, Fallon.'

Vejar corrected him. 'Two saddle-bags.'

'Which means that, if she was making a deposit, it would be a tidy sum of money,' Harker pondered.

'Yes.'

'So Klugg would be robbing a bank that holds his own money,' Harker said doubtfully.

'Money he's robbed from another bank,' Vejar cynically clarified the situation.

'That figures,' the sheriff conceded. 'Yancey

has seen the last of this woman, seeing as how she's done her job?'

'No,' Vejar replied. 'When the time comes to hit the bank she'll be there in the thick of the gunsmoke.'

'And she's the reason you don't want to back me against Klugg and his gang,' Harker guessed shrewdly.

Not answering this, an image of Gloria Malone sprang into Vejan's mind. He had known many women in his time but, Raya excepted, none of them could compare with the black-haired outlaw. There was something vibrantly alive about everything she did, all that she said. If there was a way to protect her when Klugg rode into town, then he would find it and use it.

Forcing the mental picture from his head, Vejar said, 'The thing is, George, Klugg will soon be riding into town, and you've got to move fast if you're going to stop him.'

'You know how this outlaw operates, Fallon, so I'd be loco not to seek your advice.'

'It is important that you don't let Klugg into town,' Vejar instructed. 'Once inside he'll use any trick, no matter who gets hurt. For a start you'll need enough men to cover each end of the street so that no one can enter the town.'

Getting up from his chair and buckling on his

41

gunbelt, Harker walked over to unlock the chain of the gun rack and select a rifle. He told Vejar, 'Right now I'm going to ride out to the Lazy J, Fallon. Jim Reynard has some tough hands working for him.'

'Gunslingers?' Vejar queried.

'Cowboys,' Harker answered. 'But they're a rough bunch. Jim will let me borrow ten.'

'Make it fifteen,' Vejar advised.

Nodding assent, Harker said, 'First though, I'll call at the bank and ask Hiram what business your woman did there this morning.'

'Not my woman, George.'

Dan Matthews always became uneasy whenever George Harker was out of town. The town council had just two reasons for making Dan deputy sheriff: the first was that the wages were so poor that no one else wanted the job, and the second, that Yancey had been practically crime free since Fallon Vejar had lit out.

Having been called to the Hero of Alamo that evening, he liked even less having sole responsibility for keeping law and order. A boy had been sent to him with a message that Ben Poole was in the saloon, liquored-up and likely to explode into violence at any moment. Dan couldn't imagine what anyone thought that he could do against the brutish Ben Poole. But he had to

42

show willing in order to keep his deputy's badge and his pittance of an income.

It disappointed Dan to find the saloon was far from crowded. The more people there, the greater would be the chance of someone coming to his aid if Ben Poole started on him. Yancey was accustomed to the youngest Poole brother's regular bouts of drunken violence, which George Harker usually took care of with consummate ease.

But George wasn't here right now, and Ben, who had shoulders like an ox, had struck a challenging pose. Back to the bar, both elbows resting on it, his thick, black, wavy hair was brushed back from a forehead so low that just a narrow strip of skin separated the hair from the bushing eyebrows. In his rumbling voice he was taunting the half-circle of men who had left a clear space round him.

Approaching the bruiser, but careful to stay at more than an arm's length away from him, old Dan said in a shaky voice, 'Now then, Ben, nobody here is looking for trouble.'

'Maybe you ain't looking for it, old man, but you just found it,' Ben snarled, pushing himself forwards from the bar.

Knees knocking together, Dan considered forgetting both his badge and his wage, and making a run for it. But relief flooded through him as he heard the batwing doors open behind him, and Ben switched his angry glare from him to whoever had just come into the saloon. A square-toothed grin of delight split Ben Poole's flat face almost in two.

Sensing the tension inside the saloon while still outside, Vejar eased his .45 in its holster before entering cautiously. Once he was inside, Dan Matthews came hurrying towards him on legs so bent that he rolled with each step, The old fellow's body was no thicker than wire, with the clothes he wore hanging on it. The ancient man was looking at him anxiously through eyes that leaked tears that owed everything to age and nothing to sadness.

Opening his mouth to speak, the old face imploded, leaving on display a toothless upper gum and a row of black and brown snaggly teeth in his lower jaw. 'Am I glad you're here, Fallon. Ben Poole is acting up right ornery again.'

The oldster had no time to say anything more, as Ben Poole advanced on Vejar. He walked with quick, short steps, the weight of his body shifting rhythmically to either heel. With a slight swagger to it that was a challenge in itself, it was the walk of a self-assured fighting man.

Poole sneered, 'Well, well! There stands the cowardly back-shooter.'

'I came in here for a drink, Poole,' Vejar said. 'Not to seek trouble.'

'Brother Billy wasn't looking for no trouble when you shot him in the back, Vejar.'

As he finished speaking, Poole threw off his coat and slipped out of his checkered shirt. There were gasps of admiration from the onlookers as he stood there in a scarlet under-shirt that showed off his muscle-packed body to advantage.

'Back off, Poole.'

Deaf to Vejar's warning, Ben Poole moved forward with both arms spread wide, his hands open. 'I'm unarmed, Vejar, and I sure ain't going to give you a chance to shoot me when I gets the better of you.'

Though quiet up to that moment, the saloon somehow produced a kind of magical silence. The air was charged with expectancy. Glancing round to double-check that the other two Poole brothers were not among the crowd, Vejar unbuckled his gunbelt, rolled it around the holstered gun, and passed it to a shaking Dan Matthews.

As Vejar stepped forwards, his powerful physique, though much lighter than Poole's, was enhanced by gracefulness. A murmur rippled through the crowd, for there was a majesty about the two men. There was a primitive glory in a scene that had fearless gladiators facing each other, ready for combat.

Ben Poole was known as a hardhitter and, when the fight began, Vejar sparred on the defensive as his giant opponent circled him looking for an opportunity to close. Aware that he could not match Poole in strength, Vejar knew that he must use cunning to gain an advantage. Deliberately creating a false opening, he was gratified when the gullible Poole rushed in. Relying on his speed, Vejar moved fast, extremely fast. As Poole surged forwards on the attack, he agilely ducked, took a short side step and did a violent half turn to drive his elbow hard into Poole's midriff.

Feeling ribs crack as his elbow drove in, Vejar turned as Poole's breath escaped from him in an angry, hissing eruption. Turning to face Poole again, who was slightly bent forward, holding his ribs and stomach with both hands, Vejar delivered a rapid series of fast punches to Poole's big face; left and right, left and right. His knuckles ripped open a long gash in Poole's cheek. A power-packed blow from Vejar's right hand completely split open Poole's top lip right up to the nostril. Shaking his huge head, causing the two halves of his cut lip to flap and spray blood in all directions, Ben Poole brought up both hands to protect his terribly damaged face.

Without a pause, Vejar changed tactics to launch a two-fisted attack on Poole's body. Groaning in pain, the huge man brought his arms down again to defend his body. As Poole's left arm came down, Vejar crossed it with a right-hand punch that landed on his adversary's prominent brow, opening up a red, blood-gushing gash over the left eye.

Poole took several steps backwards, and only colliding with the bar kept him upright. Some of the crowd, courageous at seeing the dangerous bully reeling all but helpless, started to cheer Vejar on as he stepped up to knock Poole's head to the right with one punch, then knock it to the left with a blow from his other hand. Concentrating on ending the fight by completely demolishing his huge opponent, Vejar was oblivious to a sudden silence that descended on the crowd. Consequently, he didn't know that Ben Poole's two brothers had just entered the saloon.

Something smashed against the back of his head, and the next he knew was that he was lying on the floor. Lew Poole was standing on one side of him and Michael Poole on the other. Both brothers were delivering vicious kicks to his head and body.

The knowledge that he was about to be kicked to death galvanized the groggy Vejar into action.

Using his left elbow to gain leverage, he rolled swiftly to his right, grabbing Lew Poole's right ankle with both hands as he went. A tug from Vejar unbalanced Lew Poole, who staggered awkwardly but didn't go down. But the diversion permitted Vejar to keep rolling and come up shakily on to his feet.

Michael Poole was on him in a flash. The tall, lean Poole brother let go with a punch that caught Vejar flush on his left eye. The force of the punch sent Vejar flying backwards, he hit a table, overturning it as he crashed to the wooden floor. Coming up fast, he saw Michael Poole moving in on him, throwing another mighty punch. Vejar hoisted the table by its legs. Unable to stop the punch he was throwing, the tall Poole brother yelled out in pain as his fist crashed into the tabletop, crunching the bones of his hand.

With his left eye rapidly closing, Vejar lunged at Michael Poole, who was holding his damaged hand, his face twisted in agony. He was unable to defend himself, and Vejar felled him with a terrific right-hand punch.

Out of the fight completely, Michael Poole lay unconscious on the floor. But his brother Lew came up on Vejar's blind side, using a bottle to club him to the floor. Fighting to remain conscious, Vejar scrambled away from the kicks Lew Poole was aiming at him. He rose up, ready to deal with Lew, but Ben Poole, his face a bloody pulp, came up behind Vejar to catch him in a bear hug, pinioning his arms to his sides.

Grinning happily, Lew Poole stepped forward to smash punch after punch at the helpless Vejar. With blood from cuts inflicted by the punches completing his blindness, Vejar slumped and would have fallen if Ben Poole hadn't been holding him.

Exhausted by the non-stop battering he was giving Vejar, Lew Poole stopped and nodded to his brother, who let Vejar drop to the floor. Peering up one-eyed through a veil of blood, Vejar saw Ben Poole drawing his gun, aiming it at him.

'You lived like a dog, Vejar,' Lew Poole snarled. 'Now you can die like a dog.'

Cursing his stupidity in taking off his gunbelt in the first place, Vejar was watching Poole squeeze the trigger, when a shot rang out. Staggering sideways, Lew Poole dropped his gun and clapped his hand to his neck. A bullet had grazed him, drawing blood but otherwise causing no real injury.

Unable to believe his luck, Vejar saw a smile tweak at the corners of Dan Matthews' mouth. Then George Harker was reaching down to put

a hand in Vejar's armpit and pull him to his feet.
'I guess that you'll have company in the jailhouse tonight, Fallon,' the sheriff quipped.

FOUR

'So you've heard of George Harker, Ken?'

Gloria Malone asked the question as she sat in brilliant noon sunshine, cleaning and oiling her handgun. The gang had taken over an abandoned line shack in the foothills some thirty miles from Yancey. The shack stood on a grassy rise, alone and as desolate as a desert island. When she had told Klugg the name of Yancey's sheriff, Gloria had noticed that the outlaw had shown not fear, which would have been out of character, but a certain apprehension that intrigued her. This Harker had to be some *hombre* to make Ken Klugg react in that way.

Not answering until his daily period of quick-draw practice had been completed, Ken Klugg holstered his .45 and walked over to sit beside her on the grass close to one side of the shack.

'You must be the only one who's never heard of Harker, Gloria,' he remarked.

'He's that good?'

'Better than good, much better.'

'How does that affect our plan for Yancey?' Gloria enquired.

She waited for a reply that she suspected would never come. Klugg had become unfriendly towards her in their present situation. She missed Fallon Vejar terribly. Since Vejar had left, Klugg had been trying to get closer to her. Having repelled him every time he made a move, she knew that he had grown increasingly angry at being rejected. She guessed it would have resulted in a showdown between them before now, except for the fact she had filled Vejar's position as the most valuable member of the gang. Klugg just couldn't afford to lose her. The other four, though competent with firearms and not lacking in courage, were incapable of performing without supervision. Maybe that wasn't true of Richie Deere, the youngest of them, a kid who had become Vejar's protégé, and who had been morose from the moment Vejar, his friend and idol, had ridden out.

'The only difference it makes,' Klugg said, surprising her by replying to her query, 'is that we take Sheriff Harker out before we hit the bank. The kid can take care of Harker.'

Gloria was startled then, as Klugg turned his upper body, drawing his gun as he did so. In the stillness the sound when he fired the peacemaker was ear-splitting. Klugg had returned his gun to its holster in a fluid movement when Gloria turned her head to look over her shoulder. A gopher that had been innocently sneaking past some yards behind them, was now splattered bloodily over the grass, completely shattered by Klugg's bullet. Impressed by Klugg's speed, Gloria was astounded by the fact that in a split second he had either heard or sensed the small creature behind him, and had known its exact position. It was a frightening reminder of what a dangerous man Ken Klugg was.

'Just keeping the eye and the hand in,' he smilingly explained, patting his holstered gun.

Worried by the thought of Richie Deere, a complex but nevertheless likeable kid, going up against a sheriff renowned for his fast draw, Gloria said, 'Obviously you could face this George Harker, Ken, but surely young Richie isn't up to it?'

'Face Harker?' Klugg chuckled. 'I'm not going to ask the kid to *face* the sheriff, Gloria. I can't risk losing Deere before hitting the bank.'

Getting the message, that Richie would simply wait in the shadows to dry gulch the sheriff, Gloria said, 'That's a relief. Yancey is a lively place, Ken, and it will take all of us to pull off the raid.'

'That's why I need to know more about the place before I send the kid to get Harker.'

'Sounds to me that I'll soon be riding back into Yancey all on my lonesome,' Gloria commented drily.

Taking Gloria's sketch of the layout of Yancey's bank from his pocket, Klugg studied it before saying, 'You did fine with this, Gloria, and meeting the sheriff's girl sure was lucky. Go back to Yancey and make some excuse to see that girl. Find out from her how many deputies Harker can call on, and if Vejar will be backing the sheriff.'

'I'll ride out at first light,' Gloria told him, but Klugg shook his head.

'You'll leave for Yancey right now,' he ordered. 'If Vejar's warned the town that we're coming, then we have to hit them before they can organize a defence. You ride out now, and be back here before sundown tomorrow with a full report.'

Stretched out on a cot in the cell that had become his home, a cut and bruised Vejar winced as Raya gently bathed his battered face. As George Harker had stayed with them since he'd brought her in to tend his wounds, Vejar and Raya had had little chance of any real conversation. The reunion between him and the girl had been a non-event, with Raya embarrassed and strangely detached. Every word that they spoke to each other was self-censored due to Harker being present. If the sheriff sensed the strange atmosphere, he certainly didn't show it.

The three of them were the sole occupants of the jailhouse. Not wanting to tie himself down with prisoners at such a time, Harker had not arrested the Poole brothers. After helping the badly beaten Vejar from the saloon to the jailhouse the previous night, a disappointed George Harker reported that the Lazy J ranch was busy with a roundup ready for a trail drive, and the owner could spare him only six men.

'That's not enough, George,' Vejar had warned.

'It's all I've got,' the sheriff had replied resignedly. 'There would be no problem if you were with me, Fallon.'

'That's not possible, George. I'll stick around long enough to see you set up right to take care of Klugg, then I'll be riding out.'

'The way you spoke had me real certain that you owed Klugg no loyalty.'

'I don't,' had been Vejar's response. He saw no reason to explain that he couldn't draw his gun against Gloria Malone or against Richie Deere, a hero-worshipping kid who had become his friend.

The sheriff brought up the subject of Gloria now, as Raya's first aid came to an end. Holding the bowl of water in which Raya had constantly rinsed the cloth she was using, he said, 'I reckon as how you were mistaken about that woman, Fallon. Hiram says some woman did open an account yesterday, but her name was Carmel Morrow.'

'That's right,' Raya agreed. 'I met her yesterday. Carmel and her brother are looking to buy a place around here. She seems a very nice person.'

'I'm sure that the woman I saw coming out of the bank was Gloria Malone,' Vejar protested.

'It couldn't have been her, Fallon.' Harker was adamant. 'Hiram required certain documentation before he would agree to opening an account, and the paperwork produced by the woman was in the names of her and her brother, Carmel and Alan Morrow.'

'That's the way Klugg works,' Vejar sighed. 'He plans every job meticulously. The time Gloria would have spent doing that business in the bank, means she took every detail of the place away with her.'

Packing her utensils into a bag, Raya enquired, 'Is there something going on that I don't know about?'

'Nothing that you need to know, Raya,'

Harker assured her. 'It's something Fallon mentioned that I felt that I should keep an eye on.'

Satisfied by this, Raya shyly bade Vejar farewell. Thanking her for tending his injuries, he turned away to avoid seeing her raise up on tiptoe to kiss Harker on the cheek. Closing the door behind her, Harker returned to stand looking down at Vejar.

'In a couple of days you'll have recovered, be fighting fit,' the sheriff predicted. 'You're sure that you won't stay in Yancey to help me and my six cowboys fix that band of outlaws real good?'

Causing himself pain by shaking his head, Vejar said, 'Sorry, *amigo*, That's something I just can't do.'

It was late afternoon and the sun had lost its ferocity as Raya Kennedy made her way home from the jailhouse. Welcoming the new coolness, breathing fresh air deeply, she was paying little attention to her surroundings until her name was called.

'Raya! We meet again.'

Smiling delightedly, Carmel Morrow had opened the door of Wu Chua's staid little teahouse from the inside and was standing in the doorway.

'Carmel, it's good to see you back in town,'

Raya responded, walking towards her recently acquired friend. 'Have you and your brother found a place?'

'Not exactly. Let me get you a cup of tea, and I'll tell you all about it.'

Accepting the invitation, Raya went in and the smiling Chinese proprietor pulled out a chair for her to be seated across a little table from Carmel, It surprised Raya that, up close, Carmel's beauty was based on the irregularity of her features. She had a high-bridged nose, cheekbones that were too pronounced, a mouth that was exceptionally wide, too long white teeth, and lips that were provocatively but unusually thick. But this was a stunning combination.

'How are you, Missy Raya?' the Chinese man enquired.

'I'm very well, Mr Chua, thank you,' Raya answered. 'And how is your good self.'

'Mighty fine, Missy Raya, mighty fine.' The Chinaman used an Americanism in reply as he left to fill the new order placed by Carmel.

She smiled across the table at Raya. 'You are obviously well known and very respected in Yancey.'

'As I said, Carmel, I have lived here all my life,'

'Nothing to do with being betrothed to the sheriff?' Carmel questioned, with a twinkle of amusement in her dark-brown eyes. She was a fun person. 'After all, he must be an important person in a thriving town like Yancey.'

This time it was Raya who chuckled. 'Hardly. Possibly because of George's reputation, the town has very little crime. He runs things single-handed, unless his only deputy, a frail old man, is taken into account.'

'Nevertheless, he can surely call on volunteers in the unlikely event of something serious happening,' Carmel suggested.

The naïvety of what Carmel had said brought a sweet smile to Raya's face. 'The people of Yancey are business folk, not gunfighters, Carmel. Anyway, nothing that George can't take care of will ever happen.'

'Of course not,' Carmel agreed.

They fell silent for a few moments as Mr Chua returned with a tray and poured tea for them from an intricately decorated teapot. Carmel restarted the conversation by holding her cup ready to clink it against Raya's, saying 'Let's drink to our friendship.'

Giggling, Raya responded with, 'To a long friendship. Have you found a ranch that you'd like to buy?'

'There is one place that we are going to look at tomorrow,' Carmel replied. 'I'm undecided about it, so I intend to let my brother make the final decision.'

'Probably wise,' Raya agreed.

'We could have settled it today, but Alan is busy with branding the stock at the ranch of a friend we are staying with.' Carmel explained. 'My brother puts work above all else, but he has promised to take time off tomorrow so that we can see our prospective new home together.'

There was a pause in their conversation then. Wu Chua, who was clearing cups and saucers from a table close to them, took advantage of it. 'Excuse me, Missy Raya. I saw you coming from the jail, and wondered if that man was badly hurt in the saloon fight last night?'

'No, thank the Lord,' Raya replied. 'Just some cuts and bruises that I treated as best I could. He'll soon be up and about again.'

'I am very glad, Missy Raya,' the Chinaman said, moving off with a loaded tray.

Curiosity creasing her brow, Carmel asked, 'Are you a nurse, Raya?'

'Good heavens, no,' Raya said, with a self-conscious laugh. 'I'm not capable of something like that. I'm a dressmaker. My friend Mary and I are partners in a little business of our own.'

'That's nice,' Carmel said. 'You'll definitely have a new customer once I've settled. We haven't known each other long enough for me to ask a personal question, so forgive me if I am overstepping the mark. Why would a dressmaker be tending the wounds of a man in jail?'

'It's complicated,' Raya said awkwardly.

'Then say no more. I had no right to pry, Raya.'

Raya contemplatively studied the pattern on her cup. 'I don't mind at all, but it is difficult to explain. You see, Fallon, the man who was hurt, is not in jail. He is a friend of George and myself, who has just come back into town.'

'A friend who is going to replace the ancient deputy sheriff you told me about?'

'Oh dear no,' Raya responded, blushing a deep red. 'This embarrasses me. You see, this man, Fallon and I were once to have been married. Things went wrong and he left town. The situation is such that he could never work with George.'

'I can understand why,' Carmel said. She pouted exaggeratedly, chiding Raya playfully. 'You are a dark horse, Raya. So much romance in your life.'

'You must think me awful,' Raya said, ruefully.

'Of course not. It's because you are such a pretty girl,' Carmel complimented her. 'Now, I must be on my way, as I want to get back to the ranch before dark.'

'I'll see you again?' Raya queried worriedly.

'You can count on it, Raya. I've got this feeling that we are going to be good friends.'

'I really do hope so, Carmel.'

*

'How many outlaws are there in this gang, George?' Walter Randall asked.

'Six including Ken Klugg, the leader,' the sheriff replied, from where he sat on a sackful of alfalfa.

The impromptu meeting of the town council was being held in the rear room of Randall's general store. Harker had called the councillors together to tell them of the planned raid on the bank, and to explain how he intended to protect the town.

'Just one point, George.' A frowning Hiram Anstey raised a hand to stop the three other councillors, all of whom were trying to speak at once. 'Am I right in thinking that all the information you have about this planned raid on my bank came from Fallon Vejar.'

'That is correct, Hiram.'

'Vejar is hardly a model citizen,' complained Henry Drake, who owned Yancey's livery stables.

John Thurston, the town's doctor, went further in condemnation of Vejar. 'That man is nothing but a damned outlaw himself, Harker.'

'That is true, Doc,' Harker conceded. 'In fact, up to a few days ago he was riding with the Klugg gang.'

'What?' the doctor snorted in disgust. 'Where

is the damned fellow now?'

'In the jail,' Harker said.

'Best place for that scoundrel,' Walter Randall opined, and the other councillors voiced their agreement enthusiastically.

'He's not a prisoner,' Harker informed them. 'He's just sleeping in the jail because Ma Cousin's place is closed.'

'Hogwash! There are rooms vacant at my hotel,' Joseph Behm pointed out.

'I reckon Fallon didn't want to pay your tariffs, Joe,' the sheriff commented wryly.

Picking up a claw hammer, Walter Randall banged it on the table like a judge with his gavel. 'I call this meeting to order.'

'You sceered me half to death with that racket, Walter,' Henuy Drake protested.

'It's this whole caboodle that has me afeared,' Randall countered. 'Tell me, Sheriff Harker, how do we know that this Vejar isn't in town to set up the raid?'

'Because I say he's not,' Harker replied.

'That's good enough for me,' Hiram Anstey said.

'And me,' Henry Drake agreed. 'George deserves our backing on this.'

'And I'll go along with you, providing Vejar doesn't play any part in protecting our town,' Walter Randall stipulated.

Harker shocked them with an announcement. 'I asked Vejar to do so, but he won't. Yancey could well do with a man like Fallon Vejar right now.'

'I can't agree with that,' Dr Thurston said firmly.

'Neither can I,' Randall muttered grumpily. 'You have your deputy, Dan Matthews, Sheriff, so what is your plan.'

'You don't pay old Dan enough for me to let him risk his life, Walter,' Harker answered. 'Dan will be a lookout at Macadam Point. He'll be able to ride back in and warn me that Klugg is on his way to town, then Dan will take himself home and stay there. That will allow me at least half an hour to prepare for the gang's arrival. I'm borrowing six men off Jim Reynard out at the Lazy J. That's all Jim can spare me this time of year. All I can do is have three of them under cover at each end of the street.'

'And you'll be at the bank, George?' Hiram Anstey checked nervously.

'I won't let you down, Hiram.'

'You don't have to tell me that, George.'

'Is there anything that we can do to help, George?' Henry Drake enquired.

'Thanks for the offer, Henry,' Harker said. 'But I want all four of you to keep yourselves and everyone else out of harm's way. As soon as I give the warning that Klugg and his band are heading for town, take all the women and children and put them in the school.'

'Is it likely to be that bad?' Randall asked tremulously.

'Where Klugg's concerned it would be foolish not to expect the very worst,' Harker advised.

'I must say that this business has me worried, George,' Hiram Anstey admitted.

'You are not on your own in that, Hiram,' Sheriff George Harker confessed.

FIVE

The five of them sat round the shack's crude table eating bacon and beans that Gloria had prepared reluctantly. As the only woman among the outlaws she was expected to cook for the others and clean the dirty dishes afterwards. That was something she resented. Except for Klugg himself, she was the fastest gun and a better shot than any of them. That being so, she objected to having to do such menial chores. However, it would be plumb crazy to take a head-on protest to Ken Klugg. Maybe after the bank job at Yancey she would make a stand, somehow establish her rights as Klugg's second-in-command. Nerves wouldn't be so strained then as they were now, and the outlaw boss might well be swayed by her quiet rebellion.

Finishing his meal, Klugg took out and studied a pocket watch that he stolen from a passenger during a train hold-up. First sucking noisily on his teeth, he then said to Richie Deere, 'You head off once you've cleared that plate, kid. It will be dark by the time you ride into Yancey. That'll give you the whole evening to set up what you have to do.'

The kid raised his head of black curls, his youthful, good-looking face expressionless as he stared unafraid at the intimidating outlaw boss and said, 'It ain't my way to go sneaking about in the darkness, Klugg, shooting a man without warning. You wouldn't ask Fallon Vejar to shoot a man down like a dog.'

'Vejar isn't here, so I'm not asking him, and I sure as hell aren't asking you, kid. I'm *telling* you. Now, eat up and hightail it out of here.'

With the kid appearing ready to argue further, fear for his safety made Gloria intervene. 'It's got to be done, Richie. There isn't one of us here who doesn't badly need that money in the bank at Yancey. With Harker out of the way the town will be wide open.'

'I knows that,' the kid acknowledged, 'but I can face that sheriff or anyone else man-to-man, Gloria.'

'Nobody doubts that, Richie, but there's too much at stake for any of us to take risks,' Gloria pointed out. Being aware of the hero worship problem the kid had, she added, 'Fallon knows that you would want to call the sheriff out,

Richie, and that you got what it takes to beat George Harker to the draw.'

Close to being pacified by this, the kid had one final question for her. 'Are you right sure that Fallon will understand when he hears about it?'

'I'm absolutely certain that he will, Richie.'

To her relief, the kid cleaned his plate and then stood up despondently to buckle on his gunbelt, reach for his rifle and shrug into his coat. The cold way in which Klugg watched the kid as he went out of the door confirmed Gloria's worst fear. If the kid had objected further, then the outlaw boss would have shot him right there in the shack, without compunction.

'That's Harker taken care of,' a satisfied Klugg said to Gloria, when Richie Deere had closed the shack door behind him. 'This girl in Yancey is certain about Vejar not backing Harker?'

'Absolutely,' Gloria said, with an emphatic nod. 'Vejar will never forgive Harker for taking her from him.'

'What about when Harker is no longer on the scene?'

'I don't understand, Ken?'

'Vejar comes from Yancey, so what I'm asking is whether he's likely to help the townsfolk when they have no sheriff to protect them?'

'The last thing they'd want is help from Vejar,' Gloria assured Klugg. 'He's an outcast, Ken. A man they would never trust.'

'Good,' Klugg said.

One of the other two outlaws, a scar-faced mulatto known only by the single name of Jack, with an immediate ancestry so abstruse that even he was unsure of it, spoke up truculently. 'You've been doing a lot of talking, Klugg. When do you stop talking and we all start doing?'

'Are you looking to run things, Jack?' Klugg asked, in a deceptively casual tone.

Tension among them always built to a dangerous level immediately prior to a robbery. It had grown even worse of late. Gloria guessed they all realized that after so many years on the outlaw trail, virtually untouched by the law, they were pushing their luck to the edge of an abyss of disaster. The chances of the next raid being their last was greater each time. The atmosphere in the shack was now so taut that she was nervous about intervening. But Mitchell Staley, the remaining outlaw, and a surprisingly mild-mannered, gentle man saved her from doing so.

Recognizing that Jack was provoking the volatile Klugg, Staley spoke up. 'There's no call to get riled up, Ken. Jack's just anxious to get some of that Yancey money in his pocket.'

'As we all are,' Gloria said, as a contribution

towards keeping the peace.

Though still holding Jack in a steely gaze, Klugg's aggression abated. He addressed all three of them. 'We need to make some changes. Without Fallon Vejar, our usual tactics won't work at Yancey. We'll run through how to manage with a man short in the morning, but even then we may have to alter things when we get to town.'

'Why should that be, when the sheriff won't give us any trouble and there is no real deputy?' Gloria asked.

'We are going to hit what is probably the wealthiest bank in the territory, Gloria,' Klugg explained. 'Even the most craven coward in Yancey won't let us walk away with his money unopposed. We could find ourselves up against a citizens' committee blasting away with scatter-guns, and there is only five of us now.'

'I was only asking out of interest, not criticizing,' Gloria said.

That was true. For all his many faults, Ken Klugg was a man whom Gloria could follow with a wordless faith. He was a natural-born leader. If serving in any army he would have risen to the rank of general. A brilliantly fast thinker, who on occasions when they had been pinned down under a hail of lead, had instantly come up with a plan that succeeded in them getting away from town unscathed and with the proceeds from a raid intact.

'If any of you have any more questions, save them until the morning,' Klugg advised. His head drooped like a tired horse, and he appeared to be staring at something that Gloria and the others couldn't see.

All three of them knew their leader well enough to accept that this was a time to stay silent.

It was payday at the local ranches, and the saloon was full of noise and movement that night. The gambling tables were frantically busy, and half-drunken cowboys were enthusiastically jumping and foot-stamping around in what they consid-ered to be dancing with less enthusiastic but sweating saloon girls. Fallon Vejar, his damaged face healing so that the injuries were hardly noticeable in the saloon's flickering lighting, stood apart from the festivities, drinking at the bar with Sheriff Harker.

Using a thumb to indicate the boisterous crowd, Harker said, 'Normally this is as bad as it gets in Yancey, Fallon. Before this night is over I'll probably have to crack a few skulls and lock up one or two would-be hard men, but that's it. So you can understand why I'd prefer not to have this bank raid about to spoil the quiet life for me.'

'The quiet life wouldn't have suited you at one time, George,' Vejar reminded his friend. 'Maybe it's time you were stretched, just so you keep the old reflexes in working order.'

'We were both wild ones in our day,' Harker agreed. He did so looking straight ahead as if addressing the whole world and not Vejar in particular. 'But right now I sure am ready to settle down.'

This sent a shaft of emotional pain through Vejar. George Harker would be settling down with Raya, who, for Vejar, was a dream that now would never be realized. Though he had forced himself to accept this since his return to Yancey, it still didn't sit easily with him. Had his rival been anyone but George Harker, then things would be different, very different.

'Whether you settle down with your memories, or have them ride the trail with you, George, they make sure that you never sleep good,' Vejar said.

'I've found myself a new philosophy,' a slightly embarrassed Harker confided in Vejar. 'I intend to build myself a whole new batch of happy memories to kill off the old bad ones.'

'I sure hope that works, George.'

Draining his glass, the sheriff made no comment, but said, 'When trouble breaks out it will be in this place, but I'd better look in on the two other saloons before the night is much older. Do you want to tag along, Fallon, even though it may mean you get caught up in any bother that comes my way? Right now there is no way of telling where your allegiance lies, *amigo*, and that worries me.'

'I'll walk with you, George,' Vejar replied, adding, 'And if it was any gang other than Klugg's outfit, I'd be standing right at your side when the bank is hit.'

Harker made no reply as they headed to the door together and went out into the night. They turned right, heading for the Ace of Spades saloon. The sheriff strolled unhurried and unworried, but the thought that the Poole brothers could be lurking anywhere in the shadows made Vejar vigilant. Bent on vengeance, they had a cunning that made them formidable foes.

When he and Harker were about halfway between the two saloons, he sensed that something was amiss. He slowed, edging in close to the wall of the building they were passing. Moving nearer to him, Harker whispered a question, 'What's up?'

'I'm not sure, George.'

'The Pooles?'

'Could be,' Vejar whispered back, as he tried to identify what had disturbed him. Had it been a furtive movement, or the click of the hammer being thumbed back on a six-shooter? He stood motionless. The night was cool, overcast, but he felt a quick dampness on the back of his shirt.

Vejar took stock of their surroundings. The street up ahead was illuminated enough by the lights of Joseph Behm's hotel to satisfy Vejar that it presented no problem. The two-storey building across the street was in darkness. A parapet about eighteen inches high ran along the front edge of the building's flat roof, and Vejar studied it for any irregularity in its shape that would indicate someone was crouching behind it. There was nothing unusual there.

'What do you think, Fallon?' Harker asked in a low voice.

Not answering while he studied the upper storey of the building across the street, Vejar asked, 'Who owns Ned Jessup's place over there?'

'When old Ned died, Walter Randall bought it from Ned's son. Randall uses it as a kind of warehouse for his surplus stock.'

'Does Randall use the first floor that used to be Jessup's living-quarters?' Vejar enquired.

'No, that part of the building is vacant now.'

Looking again at the two sashed windows of the upper storey, Vejar was puzzled. There was something out of place, but what it was continued to elude him. Then it clicked suddenly into his head. The horizontal frame dividing the upper and lower window on his left was a single length of wood, whereas even in the poor light he could see two lengths of wood at the division of the panes of the window on his right. He judged there was a distance of about six inches between the two frames. It must have been the sound of the window being raised that had alerted him.

He was about to convey this to Harker, when the perceptive sheriff hissed a warning. 'The upstairs window on the right is open at the bottom.'

'I've just noticed that, George. My guess is that one of the Pooles is up there.'

Reaching out to touch Vejar's arm lightly, Harker informed him, 'From here it's impossible to see, Fallon. Keep your eye on that window. I'm going to move to the right to get a better look.'

'Careful, George. The hotel lights reach to within a foot or so from us.'

'I won't move out of the shadows,' Harker reassured him. 'But cover me, Fallon.'

Drawing his .45, Vejar lined it up on the top window as he heard the sheriff's furtive movements. He called in a hoarse whisper, 'Can you see anything, George?'

'No,' came Harker's reply. 'If there's a Poole up there, then he's well—'

The sharp crack of a rifle brought an end to the sheriff's sentence. Firing at the flash he had seen up at the window, Vejar heard the glass shatter and fall tinkling to the boardwalk. Then, in the new silence, there was a heavy thud at his side and an agonized groan came from Harker. Hunkering in the darkness, he found the sheriff lying on his side with a fast-growing stain darkening the front of his shirt. He had been shot in the chest and badly wounded. Vejar was mortified that a bullet intended for him had brought down his friend.

The sound of gunfire had brought people cautiously out on to the street. Unaware of the danger he was putting himself in, Dan Matthews came running wheezily up to Vejar, asking, 'What's happened?'

Grabbing the oldster's shirt, Vejar pulled him into the shadows, saying tersely, 'George Harker's been hurt real bad. Wait till I say, then run to fetch Doc Thurston. Keep in the shadows when you go.'

Bending to make a quick check on Harker, who was still unconscious, with blood now trickling ominously from the corner of his mouth, Vejar called a muted order to Matthews 'Go, Dan, go!'

As the old man scurried away, Vejar leapt off the boardwalk and ran across the street, targeting the upstairs window with five rapid-fire shots as he went. There was no return fire.

Not slowing his pace, Vejar jumped up onto the boardwalk and hurled himself at a glazed ground-level window. While in the air, he curled up into a ball, tucking his head tight into his chest. The windowpane shattered explosively under the impact of his shoulders. Somersaulting into the room, Vejar hit the ground, rolling down an aisle between stacked boxes. Coming up into a sitting position with his back against a wooden crate, the sleeves of his shirt slashed to ribbons by the window glass, he deftly flicked the used cartridges from his Colt and reloaded it. Holding the gun in his hand, he sat for a few moments to allow his eyes to adjust to the dimness of the interior of the building.

Then he rose to his feet and began a hunt for the Poole brother who had gunned down George Harker. Aware that the man with the rifle could now be on the ground floor, Vejar moved slowly and silently along the narrow gangways between stacks of goods, in search of the stairs.

Finding the staircase in a corner of the huge room, he climbed cautiously, one step at a time. By placing most of his weight on a heavy handrail as he crept upwards, he prevented the stairs from making any sound. But he was about two-thirds from the top when a tiny creak was immediately followed by a loud crack as the wood gave a little. As still as a stone statue, Vejar waited. Within a split second a gun roared and a bullet slammed into the wooden wall behind his head. A sliver of wood sliced along his cheek, and he felt blood seeping out to run down his face.

To attempt going up would be suicidal. But Vejar wasn't prepared to wait for the man who had shot at him to come down. If he wasn't going up, then he had to find a way of getting the gunman to come down. Examining the stair rail, he discovered it was fixed securely to the actual staircase by a number of regularly spaced wooden uprights. Going down the stairs he searched the stores to find a length of thick rope. Throwing one end of the rope up over the rail, he caught it coming down and pulled it until both ends were level. Holding the ends together, he backed across the room until there was no slack in the doubled rope. His plan was to pull on the rail to make the staircase collapse. When the man upstairs heard the wood cracking, he would realize what was happening. He would be forced to come down to avoid being trapped on the upper floor.

Yet the plan would put Vejar in jeopardy. He would need both of his hands and all of his strength if he was to wreck the staircase. That meant holstering his .45.

Exploring with his feet in the gloom, he located a step to brace them against. Then he strained, pulling hard on the rope. But, despite his efforts, the stair rail held fast. Leaning back to employ his weight so that his body was at a precarious angle, he tried again. This time there was a loud creaking, but the wooden structure remained intact. Sweating profusely and gritting his teeth, Vejar again put all of his strength into the task. He was about to admit defeat when the staircase suddenly broke away from the wall.

It happened so fast that Vejar lost his balance when the rope went slack. First tottering backwards, he then fell heavily. In the poor light, he saw a panicking figure starting to descend the disintegrating stairs. The man fired a handgun and Vejar's neck burned as a bullet grazed it. Pulling himself up on to his feet, Vejar drew his gun and fired. He saw his target drop sideways and crash to the floor just as the staircase collapsed noisily in a cloud of dust.

Needing to know that his adversary was dead, and curious as to which of the Poole brothers it was, Vejar hurried across the floor and dropped to one knee beside the inert figure. Expecting to see Michael Poole, he jerked back involuntarily as he saw the sightless eyes of Richie Deere staring up at him.

Leaning against a wall, badly shaken at having killed the young outlaw whom he had grown fond of, Vejar recognized Ken Klugg's thinking behind what had just occurred. Klugg had sent the kid into Yancey to gun down the sheriff, thereby leaving the town wide open for the bank raid. Vejar and George Harker had made the mistake of thinking that one of the Poole brothers had been lying in wait for Vejar.

Bringing the sheriff to mind jolted Vejar into remembering that Harker had been in a bad way when he had left him lying on the boardwalk. Untying his bandanna, he used it to wipe the blood away from the cut on his face, and then dabbed gingerly at the groove the kid's bullet had dug along the side of his neck. Then, with a final, regretful Iook at the body of Richie Deere, he picked up the rifle that had fallen to the floor beside the kid. Then Vejar went to the window he had smashed to enter the building, and climbed out.

Brought out on to the street by the sound of gunfire, Wu Chua had insisted that the injured sheriff be carried into his sitting-room. A frantically worried Raya arrived to find George Harker stretched out on a sofa, being tended by Dr John Thurston. Lin Chua, the teashop proprietor's wife, fussed around exchanging blood-reddened bowls of water for fresh hot water as the doctor worked on the wound in Harker's chest.

Shirtsleeves rolled up, his hands and forearms red with blood, the doctor took one look at the distressed Raya and told the Chinaman, 'Take the girl out of the room, Mr Chua.'

Allowing Wu Chua to move her away, Raya refused to leave the room. She was standing by a wall, with the teashop owner's arm comfortingly round her shoulders, when the door opened and Fallon Vejar walked in. Carrying a rifle, he was a frightful sight. There was a deep gash along one side of his cheek, a bleeding bullet wound on his neck, and his shirt was in tatters.

She wanted to go to Vejar, ask him what was going on, hopefully get reassurance from him that George would be all right. But Wu Chua prevented her from doing so. She watched Vejar walk over to stand looking down at the sheriff, heard him ask, 'How is he, Doc?' Though Dr Thurston spoke too low for her to catch his words, his facial expression confirmed that she should fear the worst.

SIX

Vejar had been invited to the emergency meeting of the town council called later that night. It was, as usual, being held in the rear room of Randall's general store. When Vejar walked in, Randall, Hiram Anstey, Henry Drake, and Dr Thurston were seated side-by-side along the length of a large table. The atmosphere was solemn, but Hiram Anstey greeted him affably.

'It is good of you to come here so late at night, Fallon, particularly after what you have been through this evening.'

As Vejar acknowledged the greeting with a nod, Randall slyly slid a hand to the centre of the table, palm down. Lifting the palm, he said, 'You know what this is.'

'A tin star,' Vejar replied.

'It is a deputy sheriff's badge,' Randall corrected him, an expression of distaste at Vejar's reaction twisting his florid face.

'So?' Vejar shrugged.

'I will be surprised if Sheriff George Harker makes it through tonight,' John Thurston announced gravely.

Perturbed, Vejar said, 'I'm real sorry to hear that, Doc.'

'That is why we are asking you to be deputy sheriff,' Walter Randall said. Though not a sly man, he did, however, speak more confidently when not looking directly at the person he was addressing. He studied the ceiling, his head back a little.

'Perhaps even to become sheriff if. . . .' Diplomatically, Hiram Anstey didn't complete his sentence.

'Harker told us that you brought news of a possible bank raid here in Yancey,' Randall said. 'It seems that you know the band of outlaws concerned.'

'*Probable* bank raid,' Vejar pointed out.

'This isn't a time for word play,' Randall protested tetchily. 'The facts are that our town is under threat, and we have absolutely no way of defending it.'

'Jim Reynard's letting you have six men from the Lazy J,' Vejar reminded him. 'Barricade each end of the town, and deploy three of those men to man each of the barricades and you'll prevent the Klugg gang from entering Yancey.'

'Things have changed,' Randall told him glumly.

'Reynard was letting George Harker have his men out of friendship,' Henry Drake expanded on the subject. 'With Harker out of action, the Lazy J offer of help is no longer available. It's an extremely busy time at the ranch.'

'All we have is you and ourselves, Vejar,' John Thurston added. 'We know you feel that this town judged you badly in the past, but—'

'You don't have me,' Vejar said. 'I appreciate your difficult situation, and assure you that the past has no bearing on my decision. For personal reasons, I shall be leaving town in the morning.'

'Then all is lost,' Hiram Anstey groaned.

'I am sorry, gentlemen.'

Saying this, Vejar turned and walked out of the door. The four men left sitting at the table looked despairingly at each other. They didn't speak for some time. Then Hiram Anstey posed the question that none of them had an answer to, when he asked. 'Where does this leave us?'

'Fallon Vejar was our only hope,' Dr Thurston commented gloomily.

'Can we come up with something to change his mind?' Randall queried.

'Men like Vejar don't permit anyone to change their minds,' the doctor said. 'The only person in Yancey that Vejar is likely to listen to is George Harker.'

'And George Harker won't be around to speak to him,' Henry Drake uttered, with a long sigh.

'Exactly,' Dr Thurston said.

'At least we have until the morning to find some way to have Vejar stay in town.' Walter Randall's words sounded hopeful, but they were made worthless by the pessimism in the way he spoke them.

'If we had until domesday, then the result would be the same,' Dr Thurston predicted.

With the sun of a new day just edging up over the horizon, Fallon Vegar hitched his saddled horse to the rail outside of the jailhouse. Then he walked hesitantly towards the town's sedate teashop. His reluctance was caused by the clear memory of George Harker's lifeless appearance when he had seen him last night. He couldn't leave Yancey without bidding his old friend farewell, but he felt it unlikely that the sheriff had survived the night.

Opening the door to him, Lin Chua gave him a wan smile that gave Vejar hope until he recalled that a smile was the sweet Chinese woman's habitual expression. She ushered him into the room where Harker lay, covered by a blanket. The slight rise and fall of the cover assured Vejar that the injured man was breathing, albeit shallowly. Raya Kennedy sat on a chair beside Harker. The tired look and strain on her face eased a little at the sight of Vejar. She stood and walked to stand close to him.

'George is doing well,' she reported. 'Dr Thurston has already called in this morning. He didn't say so, of course, but I could see that he found it difficult to credit that George was still alive.'

'Have you been here all night?' Vejar asked.

'Yes.'

'What did the doc say about George this morning, Raya?'

'He said that he could make no promises,' Raya reported. 'But he did say that George is a very strong man, which is all to the good.'

'It would take more than one bullet to finish George Harker,' Vejar said, smiling at the girl. 'He'll pull through, Raya, I'm sure of that. When he's feeling better, tell him that I am sorry, but I have no choice but to leave Yancey.'

'Are you going today, Fallon?' Raya asked with a courageous smile.

'I'm leaving right now.'

'But . . .' Raya started to speak, but a sob caused her to falter. 'But George needs you. The town needs you. *I* need you, Fallon.'

She said the last four words faintly. Pondering

on the meaning behind them, Vejar then braced himself to say goodbye. He kissed her quickly and lightly on the forehead. 'Look after George, and take care of yourself, Raya.'

Reaching the door he could hear her weeping softly, but he didn't turn for fear that he would weaken. But then he was shocked into immobility as he heard George Harker's voice croak his name.

Turning his head very slowly, he saw that Raya had rushed back to crouch beside the sheriff, whose head was turned and his eyes open, looking at Vejar.

'Fallon.'

The voice was a muted croak, but it brought Vejar back to the sheriff's side. Harker's lips moved in an unsuccessful attempt at uttering more words. Then he found his voice again, but it was so feeble that Vejar had to stoop to catch what he said. 'Which one of them got me, Fallon?'

'It wasn't one of the Pooles,' Vejar told him.

'But I thought that one of the brothers was firing at you, and hit George by mistake.' Raya was badly frightened by Vejar's revelation.

Mystified, Harker struggled to find the energy to continue talking. At last, he asked hoarsely, 'Then who?'

'That bullet was intended for you, George.

Klugg sent someone into town to put you out of action before he hits the bank.'

This brought a cry of alarm from Raya. 'Then if the outlaws hear that George is alive they will make another attempt to kill him.'

'No, Raya,' Vejar said, with a negative shake of his head. 'Ken Klugg can't risk losing another man before raiding the bank.'

Realization made Harker say, 'You got the man who shot me.'

'Not a man, George, a boy. A kid named Richie Deere,' Vejar explained. 'The kid was a friend of mine.'

'Oh dear. You must feel terrible because you shot him, Fallon,' Raya gasped, tears welling up in her eyes.

With a shrug, Vejar answered, 'I feel terrible when I kill anyone, Raya, but I guess I feel it worse this time. The kid didn't deserve to die, but Klugg does for using him in the way he did.'

Having closed his eyes to recover the strength he had used up by talking, George Harker opened them again to look hopefully at Vejar. 'You've made a start against that gang, Fallon, and Yancey needs you. Walter Randall and the rest of them will probably be coming in to see me sometime today. I reckon that I could persuade them to let you take my place as the law around here.'

'They offered to make me deputy sheriff last night.'

'And?'

'You know how I'm fixed,' Vejar replied. 'I just can't go against the Klugg gang.'

Taking a quick glance at Raya, Harker said to Vejar, 'It appears to me that to take charge here is the only chance you have of protecting your friend in the gang. Money brings out the worst in those who have it and those who don't. With no law in Yancey, folk here will go to any lengths to protect their interests, and the street will run with blood. I would ask of no man that he goes against his conscience, yet if you become the law here you can keep things civilized, Fallon.'

'One man can't alter things,' Vejar said flatly.

'You aren't *one man*, you are Fallon Vejar.' Harker raised his voice in emphasis, an exercise that rapidly tired him.

To Vejar it seemed that he had already passed some invisible point of no return. George Harker was talking sense. If Vejar was running things he had a chance to foil the bank raid and maybe save the life of Gloria Malone. But it would be a momentous task, and failure on both counts couldn't be ruled out. Then there was Raya and George Harker to be considered. He couldn't ride away and leave them at this time of crisis in Yancey.

He went to speak to Harker, but the sheriff had expended all of his severely depleted energy, and had slipped into unconsciousness. Turning to Raya, Vejar said, 'When George comes round, tell him that the next time he sees me I'll be wearing a tin star.'

'Oh thank you so much, Fallon.'

A tearful but grateful Raya ran to Vejar to kiss him on the cheek. It was a kiss that held more poignancy and apprehension than it did passion. He held her for a moment. A moment too long where his feelings were concerned. They stood for a moment, aware only of each other. Then he turned and went out of the door with the fragrance of the young woman still adhering to him.

The non-return of Richie Deere had caused consternation in the outlaw camp. With both the kid's fate and the present situation in Yancey a mystery, the following morning Klugg sent Gloria into town on yet another reconnaissance mission.

Locating the only dressmaker's premises on the street, a tiny building with a small-windowed shop front, she dismounted, looked cautiously around her for a moment, then entered. Raya and another young women were standing examining a bolt of brightly coloured material.

Raya's face lit up on seeing Gloria. 'Carmel!' she exclaimed. 'What a lovely surprise. This is Mary, my friend and partner.'

'Hello.' Gloria gave Mary a friendly smile. 'I hope I'm not interrupting your work, Raya, but I was in town and thought I would call to see you.'

'I'm so glad that you did, Carmel. Was the ranch you were looking at suitable?'

'The deal's all but done,' Gloria replied. 'Now, tell me about you. Are you still doing your nursing bit?'

'Oh, you haven't heard, have you, Carmel?'

'Heard what?'

'George was shot last night.'

'The sheriff shot?' Gloria showed fake surprise and shock. 'He isn't . . . ?'

'No. He's badly hurt, but the doctor told me earlier that he will pull through.'

'Thank the Lord,' Gloria said, sighing long and loud. Then she went on, 'This is terribly selfish of me, Raya, but I put mine and Alan's money in the bank here, and now there isn't a sheriff.'

Raya said reassuringly. 'You have no need to worry, Carmel. Fallon Vejar has agreed to be the law in Yancey temporarily. Believe me, your money is as safe with Fallon as sheriff as it was when George was in charge.'

'That's good to hear.' Gloria expressed her relief. She looked flustered then. 'I'm sorry that I can't stay longer, Raya, but my brother will be worrying about me if I don't get back.'

'I understand, and it was grand seeing you, Carmel,' Raya said. 'I hope that it won't be long before you return to Yancey.'

Clasping Raya's hand, giving it an affectionate little squeeze, Gloria assured her. 'I promise you that I'll be back in town very soon.'

Raya frowned, puzzled by the strange way her friend had spoken her parting words. But she then told herself that she was being silly, and turned her attention to Mary and the business they had been discussing.

'This is my nephew, Jonathan, my sister's boy. He's willing to help you.'

Walter Randall introduced his relative to Vejar. He was young, with long black hair drooping like string from under his hat. An upbringing in business had given his narrow face the unmistakable cunning that comes from such an environment, but his thin body was alert with the tension of a hunting animal. Vejar noticed that for all his sharpness of features, the boy had impressively large and intelligent eyes.

They were standing a little way into a copse at the end of Yancey's main street, just far enough for heavy shadows to be cast. The town had a very peaceful atmosphere. Vejar found himself silently comparing it with the violence that would soon descend.

He remarked. 'You are not wearing a gunbelt, Jonathan.'

'I have never owned a gun.'

Neither have you fired one, I'll bet, Vejar thought despondently. Yet, all alone except for old Dan Matthews, he was in no position to be choosy. Though it probably had never been put to the test, the boy had the look of someone who could handle himself.

'Well,' Vejar said, 'as long as you know what you're letting yourself in for, I'll be glad of your help.'

'He won't let you down, Vejar,' Randall spoke up. 'With you to train him he'll soon be a top man with a gun.'

'There's no time for that,' Vejar exclaimed. 'Do you stock shotguns in your store, Randall?'

'The finest that money can buy.'

'Then fix up your boy with one,' Vejar instructed before he turned to the nephew. 'You don't need to be an expert with a scattergun, Jonathan. Just point it in the direction of who you want to gun down, and it's impossible to miss.'

With a nod that signalled he understood,

Jonathan said. 'I've a buddy, Len Hobart, who'd like to help out, too.'

Though appreciating two volunteers, their crass inexperience reminded Vejar of how difficult the immediate future would be. He had yet to meet Len Hobart, but he was sure to be on a par with his buddy Jonathan where guns were concerned.

Noticing his hesitation, Walter Randall advised. 'This is the best offer you'll get, Vejar. We sure appreciate you staying on to protect the bank and the town, and although we can't give you the support you need, we are doing our best.'

'You're right,' Vejar agreed. He slapped Jonathan on the shoulder. 'You've got guts, Jonathan, and I guess that your *amigo* has, too. I'll be happy to have you both along with me.'

'That's settled then,' a contented Randall said.

'It's settled, Randall. You be sure to fix up both Jonathan and his *amigo* with shotguns.'

Michael Poole strode angrily into the Twin Circle ranch house. Sitting at the table while their black maid placed cooked meals in front of them, his two brothers looked curiously up at him.

'They have insulted us and the memory of Billy,' Michael Poole complained bitterly as he

94

pulled out a chair to sit at the table.

'Who has?' Lew Poole enquired.

Remaining silent while the maid put his meal in front of him, Michael made no attempt to reply until she had left the room. Then he said, 'Randall and the others.'

'The town council?' Lew clarified what his brother had said. 'What have they done to get you so riled up, Michael?'

'George Harker got himself shot last night.'

'Dead?'

'Almost.'

'That means nothing to us,' Lew muttered, 'except that Harker won't be around to interfere when we go after Vejar.'

'That's what I was about to tell you, Lew. They've gone and made Vejar a deputy sheriff.'

A black rage blazing in his eyes, Lew Poole slammed both hands down hard on the table. The impact sent their plates flying, a cup spilled its contents on the table before rolling away to fall on the floor and shatter.

'We owe it to Billy to see that Vejar isn't a deputy for long,' Lew said. 'We wait no longer, boys. It's time to get that *mal hombre.*'

Abandoning his dinner, Ben Poole stood up. His oldest brother turned on him. 'Where are you going?'

'I'm going with you and Michael to get Vejar,'

the slow-minded Ben answered.

'Sit down and finish your dinner,' Lew told him gruffly. 'What we've got to do needs planning. You ride into town later and tell Jack Smiley that I want to see him out here pronto. Me and Michael got some thinking to do when you've gone.'

SEVEN

At Vejar's request, Walter Randall had called Yancey's citizens to a meeting in the Hero of Alamo that afternoon. Saloon business had been suspended for the event. But the good ladies of the town sniffed and snorted their disgust at entering a den of harlotry. Vejar was flanked on one side by Jonathan and by Len Hobart on the other. The latter was an overweight boy of short stature. Both young men were as yet unarmed.

Walter Randall began with a speech that caused panic when he said that a raid on the bank was imminent. Calming the crowd, Randall went on to say that the outlaw gang concerned had already shot the sheriff. There was no reaction to this, as news of George Harker's misfortune and that Vejar had killed the outlaw concerned, had spread around the town during the day. But there was a prolonged murmuring of dissent when Randall announced that Fallon

Vejar was now the law in Yancey.

Randall beckoned him, and Vejar stepped forward to address a largely hostile crowd. He said, 'It may help you to feel easier about me if I say that I'll follow Sheriff Harker's plan.'

'When is this raid supposed to happen, Vejar?' an elderly man called from the crowd.

'That's difficult to say,' Vejar replied. 'It will be soon. Most probably tomorrow.'

This shocked the assembly into a long silence. The same elderly man broke it by calling out, 'What is this plan you spoke of?'

'We need an early warning, so I will be setting Dan Matthews up as a lookout on Macadam Point. Dan will have a fast horse to get him back into town when he first catches sight of the outlaws. I estimate that will give me at least half an hour to prepare.'

'When will you be riding out with Dan to Macadam Point?'

It puzzled Vejar when he discovered that this question came from Jack Smiley, whose liking for liquor normally had him peering dumbly at the world through an alcoholic haze. But regardless who had asked the question, the townsfolk deserved to know what was happening, so he answered, 'First thing tomorrow.'

'What will the preparations you spoke of involve?' Henry Drake enquired, from where he stood at Walter Randall's side.

'Our priority must be the women and children,' Vejar said. 'When we hear that the gang is heading this way, then I want every women and child housed safely in the church until the danger is over.' He looked to where Raya stood with Mary Alcott, and called to her, 'Would you be prepared to organize that, Miss Kennedy?'

'Of course,' Raya responded self-consciously, blushing red as heads turned her way.

'Thank you,' Vejar said. 'I am sure that the ladies will co-operate fully with you.'

'That's all very well, Vejar,' Martin Frazer the town's lawyer, a small man with the nervous movements of a feeding bird, spoke up. 'But it seems as how you are on your own.'

'That is not true,' Walter Randall rebuked the lawyer. 'My nephew, Jonathan, and Len Hobart, have bravely volunteered to back Vejar.'

'That must be a great comfort to you, Vejar,' a wag shouted from the back of the crowd.

This brought laughter from the crowd to lighten the mood, but Vejar couldn't permit the courage of the two boys to be mocked. He pointed at the heckler. 'If you have the craw that Jonathan and Len have, then step forward. I'll welcome your support.'

The man who had shouted remained quiet, but Martin Frazer asked, 'You haven't said what you are going to do about it when they get here, Vejar.'

Vejar had a scheme fashioned out of desperation. He was very aware of that. Jonathan and Len, both with shotguns, would be positioned inside the bank as a last line of defence. With no knowledge of what the cunning Ken Klugg might have in mind for his attack on the bank, Vejar planned to stay loose on the street, ready for any eventuality. The realization that the lives of his two young helpers probably depended on him stopping the gang before they got to the bank, impressed on Vejar the awesome responsibility that was his. Taking out the Klugg gang single-handed would require something that bordered on a miracle.

But he couldn't share his flimsy strategy with the people of the town. He gave Frazer an evasive answer. 'I don't think it would be wise to make my arrangements public.'

Randall interrupted then to tell the assembly, 'I think that about does it, and now we should leave it to Fallon Vejar. There is just one last question. Are there any among you willing to be sworn in as deputies to assist Vejar?'

A long silence followed, interrupted only by embarrassed coughing. The middle-aged and elderly looked to the young men, who bowed their heads or turned away from the probing stares.

Unable to hide his disgust, Walter Randall declared, 'I guess that's it then. The meeting has ended, folks. May God be with you all.'

Ken Klugg's anger never showed as the animated, seething violence of most people. His wrath was a cold, calculating thing that Gloria considered was all the more terrifying. She was unable to decide whether the outlaw leader's rage was fuelled mostly by Richie Deere's failure to kill George Harker, or the fact that Fallon Vejar was now the law in Yancey. Vejar was at least Klugg's equal as a gunfighter.

Now, with a new day but an hour old, the four of them were preparing to ride into town. With Jack and Mitchell Staley out of earshot, Gloria tactfully enquired how Klugg intended to raid the bank with his depleted gang. It took him a considerable time to answer her, and when he did his reply was something that she never thought she would hear the master tactician Klugg admit.

'That can't be settled until we hit town and find out how things are there, Gloria,' the outlaw boss said with uncharacteristic uncertainty. Then he enquired, 'This girl of Vejar's?'

'She's Harker's girl,' she heard herself correcting him, surprised at the ferocity with which she did so.

The sideways glance that Klugg gave her said that he didn't like her reaction. He said, 'There is one possibility. This is just an if, a big if until we know the set-up in town, but taking her as a hostage would give us a huge advantage. From what I've heard from you, Vejar wouldn't risk her coming to any harm.'

'Probably not,' Gloria conceded reluctantly, 'but that would mean one of us guarding her, Ken, leaving just you and two others to rob the bank.'

'That wouldn't be a problem, with Vejar having to hold off because of the girl.'

Gloria had misgivings about Klugg involving Raya, a girl she had come to like. She had been uncomfortable lying to Raya about the purpose of her visits to Yancey, and the thought of the friendly girl being taken captive appalled Gloria. The worst thought of all was that Klugg would order Jack, the brooding, brutal mulatto, to abduct the girl.

'I suppose that Mitchell Staley will hold the girl,' she suggested hopefully.

'No,' he replied firmly. 'That will be your job, Gloria. You ride on in ahead of us. No one will be suspicious of a woman arriving alone in town, so you will have no problem taking this girl captive.'

'What if Vejar decides to ignore the girl and

play it his way, Ken?'

'That's a good point,' Klugg complimented her. 'You can make sure that doesn't happen by taking another woman hostage at the same time as you grab Vejar's girl. If Vejar doesn't do as we say, then you shoot the second hostage. That will show him that we mean business.'

Unable to find her voice, Gloria didn't say anything. They'd had some shoot-outs in the past with law officers and outraged citizens, but never had they carried out an inhumane act of any kind. It had to be that the problem with Fallon Vejar was warping Ken Klugg's mind.

For the first time since joining the outlaw band, Gloria Malone felt fear.

After leaving old Dan Matthews settled high on Macadam Point, Vejar had been riding for half an hour through pleasantly warm early-morning sunshine on his way back into town when some sixth sense that had never failed him, warned that he was in danger. Passing a rocky crag at the time, he accepted that he could not be a target for a rifle until he reached open terrain some thirty yards ahead. Easing his rifle in its scabbard, he was planning how to deal with what might happen when there was a hissing sound in the air close to him. Too fast for him to take evasive action, a lariat dropped over his head and shoulders. The rope was pulled tight, pinning his arms to his sides. Then a powerful tug on the lasso wrenched him backward out of the saddle. Landing painfully on the ground, Vejar heard chuckling. Looking up he saw the huge figure of Ben Poole standing on a rock. Peering down at him, Poole was holding the end of the rope and laughing gleefully.

Vejar was awkwardly trying to regain his feet when Lew and Michael Poole stepped out from behind a cluster of rocks. Grinning, they walked towards him at a leisurely pace.

'I'm real uneasy about everything,' a morbid Henry Drake admitted. 'We've got a band of outlaws about to rob our bank, and the man we're relying on to stop them was riding with them just days ago.'

'You knew that when you agreed that we should make Vejar deputy sheriff, Henry,' Walter Randall reminded him.

It was ten o'clock in the morning and they were enjoying a drink in an otherwise deserted Hero of Alamo. Having just returned from visiting George Harker, their topic of conversation was a serious one. The sheriff's injuries were no longer life threatening, but his recovery would be a slow process. Seeing the once magnificent lawman lying helplessly on a bed had depressed

Dr Thurston, Hiram Anstey and Henry Drake. Only Walter Randall appeared to be unaffected, but he was putting on a front. Like his companions, he knew that the town faced a bleak immediate future.

In an attempt to allay at least some of his colleagues' worries, Randall remarked, 'We don't have George Harker, we have to accept that, but Fallon Vejar is George's equal as a fighting man. George once confided in me that Vejar is the only man who is fast enough on the draw to worry him. When I told him that I was convinced that Vejar was a mite slower than him, George declared that if that was true, then it was so close that he was in no kind of hurry to find out.'

'I'll grant you that Vejar is probably second to none as a gunslinger,' John Thurston said. 'But the man is a maverick. He's untamed and undependable, gentleman. Can we trust him?'

'Does that question arise?' Henry Drake queried.

'I think that it does.'

Perturbed by this, Hiram Anstey asked Thurston, 'Are you thinking what I think you are thinking?'

'I am a doctor, Hiram, not a medicine man,' Thurston responded drily, 'so I don't know what you are thinking that I might be thinking.

However, your long-standing obsession with money does allow me an educated guess. Your dread is that Vejar may have come to Yancey in advance of his outlaw *compadres* to prepare the way for the bank raid.'

'Exactly,' a fearful Anstey confirmed in a choked voice.

Walter Randall rebuked the doctor and the banker. 'That sort of wild conjecture can only serve to make a bad situation worse. George Harker has total faith in Vejar, and that is good enough for me. Whether you agree with me on that or not, gentlemen, Vejar is our only hope.'

'And where is our great hope now, Walter?' Thurston challenged his friend. 'He told us himself that the outlaws were likely to ride in today. What if Dan Matthews comes riding in to say the gang is on its way – where is Vejar? No one has caught a glimpse of him all day.'

'Maybe he'll come riding in with the gang,' Anstey suggested gloomily.

'I want to put a stop to this defeatist talk right now,' Randall declared angrily. 'The nearest US marshal is a two-day ride away, and we sure ain't got two days to spare. We've got Vejar, or we've got nothing. It is up to us four to either back him or sack him, and I'm not in any doubt as to what option I'm taking.'

They looked questioningly at each other, all

three of them silent as they faced their future and its uncertainties. Then, when Henry Drake gave a curt nod, the other two joined him in agreeing with Walter Randall.

The Poole brothers had converted a back room of their ranch house into an office. There was still an hour to go before noon when they brought Vejar there. Still pinioned by Ben's lariat, Vejar was pushed onto a wooden chair and lashed to it with the spare rope of the lasso. Now Lew Poole was pacing the flagstone-covered floor, his hands behind his back and his chin resting on his chest. He gave the impression of being deep in thought, but Vejar regarded this as a charade. Lew's two brothers stood off to one side of the room.

Slowing his pacing, Lew looked sideways at Vejar. 'We Pooles have got a reputation for fair dealing hereabouts, Vejar, and we won't risk tarnishing that reputation even for a murdering crittur like you. That being so, we are going to treat you with a fairness like what you never gave to our brother Billy.'

He paused to allow Vejar to respond. When Vejar said nothing, Michael Poole spoke in support of what his eldest brother had said. 'We Pooles always plays fair.'

'What this means to you, Vejar,' Lew took up

where he had left off, 'although you sure don't deserve it, is that we are going to give you a fair trial, right here and now. Brother Michael here will represent you, look after your interests, while Brother Ben will be the prosecutor. I shall preside as judge. What is Fallon Vejar charged with, Ben?'

'Eh?' Ben Poole questioned, then shook his big head dumbly.

'What did Vejar do to Billy?' Ben asked impatiently.

'He killed Billy, murdered him.'

'So the charge is murder,' Lew said, before turning to Michael. 'How does the defendant plead?'

'Guilty,' Michael said decisively.

'I agree. Fallon Vejar,' Lew Poole gravely intoned, 'you have been found guilty of the murder of William Abraham Poole. The sentence is death.'

'Then let's get it over with,' Michael Poole urged.

Shaking his head to cancel out his brother's suggestion, Lew said, 'No. We've done this all legal like, but outsiders might think otherwise. This has to be done under cover of darkness. So we'll leave Vejar tied up here until sundown, then take him out and finish the job.'

Both Ben and Michael gave grunts of annoyance at the delay, but neither of them dared to object. All three checked Vejar's bonds before leaving. Going out of the room, with Lew carrying Vejar's gunbelt and holstered .45, they closed the heavy door behind them. Vejar, trussed so tightly that he was in pain, heard two bolts being slid home on the outside of the door.

Yancey was in a state of high tension. Dan Matthews had come riding in fast just before noon, crying out as he came that the bank robbers were heading for town. John Thurston turned a jaundiced eye on Walter Randall. The doctor asked, obviously not expecting an informative reply, 'So, Walter, where's Vejar now in our time of need?'

'I don't know any more than you do,' Randall retorted before taking command. 'But we've got to do something ourselves. Jonathan, you and Len take your shotguns and a box of shells each and get down to Hiram's bank. Conceal yourselves as best you can, making sure that you're covering the door.'

With Vejar absent, both young men were ashen-faced and visibly trembling as they obeyed Randall's orders and headed for the bank. Randall called to Henry Drake, who was standing facing the west end of the street, both hands shielding his eyes from the sun, an expression of terror rather than apprehension on his lined face.

'Henry,' Randall addressed him authoritatively, 'get yourself down the seamstress's shop and have Raya Kennedy round up the women and children and get them into the church, quick as she can.'

Within a short while the street was thronged with women dragging children by the hand as they headed for the church. Like a pretty drover in a calico dress, Raya was running this way and that, herding them in the right direction. Soon they were gone, and Henry Drake returned to his colleagues. The street was deserted except for the quartet of town councillors.

'He's done the dirty on us,' Thurston complained bitterly. 'I knew that we shouldn't have trusted Vejar.'

'Action is what we need right now, not the wisdom of hindsight,' Randall told him grumpily.

'The action I'm going to take is go take care of my bank,' Hiram Anstey said shakily.

'You do that, Hiram,' Randall concurred. 'Make good use of Jonathan and Len. They are both good lads, but they need guidance.'

'What do the three of us do?' Drake enquired.

'Get ourselves a scattergun each and wait for them varmints to get here,' Randall replied.

'Old Dan says there's only three of them.'

'That's three too many for me,' Henry Drake confessed.

'Look at it this way, Henry,' John Thurston advised, 'we're going to die before this day's out, so we just as well die as heroes.'

'I'd rather not die at all, John.'

'You don't have a . . .' the doctor began, then broke off as he looked down at the far end of town. 'Well, well, well, what have we here? Looks like a woman riding in all on her lonesome.'

'We'd best go warn her,' Randall said, starting off down the street with the others following.

Stopping her horse when they reached her, the woman looked down at them curiously. Black-haired and dark complexioned, her blouse was of blue silk, and her split riding-skirt made of the finest material. Her Stetson was off; hanging behind her on an elkskin thong that rested lightly across her smooth throat. Her deep brown eyes had a lazy sleepiness in their depths.

Disturbed by her cool appraisal, Walter Randall swatted at a fly threatening to alight on his hawk nose, and asked. 'Have you business here in Yancey, miss?'

'I've come to call on my friend Raya Kennedy,' she replied, point to Raya's small shop.

'Trouble is about to break out here, miss,'

Randall told her urgently. 'You'll find Miss Kennedy up at the church with the rest of the women. It's best that you join them and stay there until the danger is over.'

'I will take your kind advice, sir,' the woman told Randall. Then with a little thank you wave to Henry Drake who was pointing at the church, she rode on up the street.

EIGHT

Struggling uselessly against the ropes that bound him, Vejar was beset by worry that the outlaw band could already be in Yancey. His worries over Raya, George Harker, and in another respect Gloria Malone, mounted rapidly. The Pooles had chosen his prison well. Even if he could get himself free, the window was too small to squeeze through, and the door was securely bolted.

Alerted by the sound of heavy footsteps in the passageway outside, he kept still, listening. One bolt on the door was slid back. At least one of the Poole brothers had returned in no more than fifteen minutes. Why, when they didn't plan to kill him until after dark?

The second bolt was drawn, and the door opened slightly. A hand pushed the door inwards. It was a black-skinned hand, and it was holding his gunbelt. Following behind the hand was the large figure of the Pooles' black serving woman. She placed a finger to her lips for silence, which Vejar took to be a signal that the brothers were somewhere nearby.

The servant held a carving knife in her other hand. Placing Vejar's gunbelt on a small table in the corner of the room, she advanced on him, her finger still cautioning silence.

Coming close to Vejar, she whispered, 'They's going to hang you, sah, and I can no way allow that.'

Using the carving knife, the woman sawed at the ropes. When free, Vejar couldn't move because his limbs had been constricted for so long. Rubbing his arms to get life back into them, he flexed his legs over and over again until the pain had gone and he was able to stand up. The black woman waited nervously, silently urging him to keep moving and get away.

'They'll know that you released me,' Vejar said, fearing for her.

'Don't you worry about me, sah,' she assured him. 'They won't do me no harm, 'cos I'm like a mother to those boys. I tells them what to do.'

Not knowing how to express his thanks, Vejar was turning away intending to get his gunbelt, when he saw her eyes open wide with terror.

Swiftly following her gaze, he saw the lanky figure of Michael Poole standing in the open doorway, the six-shooter in his hand levelled at Vejar.

Diving to one side, Vejar hit the floor and lay flat as the terrifically loud explosion of a shot reverberated in the small room. Hearing the servant's carving knife clatter to the floor, he looked up to see her clutching her breast. Blood darkened the flowered house frock she wore, and ran freely over her hands. With no more than a small sigh, she collapsed on to the flag-stones.

Luckily for Vejar, Michael Poole was as shocked as he was by the unintentional shooting of the black woman. But, after a moment's hesitation, he pointed his gun to where Vejar was lying on the floor. With his gunbelt out of reach, Vejar rolled swiftly to one side as Poole fired and a bullet ricocheted whiningly off the flagstones. Reaching out to grasp the carving knife, he threw it just as Poole was about to squeeze the trigger again. Seeing the knife coming at him through the air, Michael Poole did a rapid half turn. An evasive move that made it seem that the knife would pass by the tall Poole brother harm-lessly.

But the sharp blade sliced through Poole's throat, opening a gash that pumped blood out like a fountain. The knife went on to bury itself in the wooden wall, creating a humming sound as it vibrated. Michael Poole's legs folded under him and he made no more sound than an after-death gurgling as he fell.

Going across the floor to the black woman, Vejar discovered that she, too, had died. Picking up his gunbelt and buckling it on, he rushed out of the room. The horse Michael Poole had ridden was hitched to a rail outside. Vejar untied the reins. He was pulling the horse around ready to mount, when Ben Poole came riding in at a gallop.

Aware that Ben must have been close enough to hear the two shots his brother had fired. Vejar accepted that his intended ride to Yancey would have to be delayed. Leaping over the rail of the veranda he backed up against the door of the house. Drawing his gun, he reached behind him to find the door was securely locked. Ben Poole expertly dismounted on the move and dropped out of sight behind a trough opposite to the door. Vejar had no cover. He backheeled the door hard, but it was sturdy and he made no impression on it.

Gun in hand, Vejar waited for Ben Poole to raise his eyes above the rim of the trough. When he did so, Poole would have the immense advantage of being a tiny, difficult target, whereas

Vejar was fully exposed. But Ben, knowing that he held the winning hand, played a waiting game that tightened Vejar's nerves to the extent that he could detect a tic fluttering at the right side of his face.

It was a situation that Vejar had concluded could not be any more desperate, when there was the crack of a rifle and the doorjamb beside his head was shredded by a bullet. Lew Poole had to be somewhere on the scene, but Vejar had no idea from which direction the bullet had come. What he did know was that he wouldn't survive if he stayed where he was for one more moment.

The top of Ben's head and his gun hand rose from behind the trough. Blasting away at Ben with his .45, Vejar ran for the horse he had abandoned a short while before. Running bent double to make himself less of a target, he saw Ben Poole duck down behind the trough. The rifle fired again and a bullet clipped the heel of Vejar's boot, the force knocking his leg from under him. Another bullet whined past him as he fell. Then he was up on his feet and running again. Aware now that Lew Poole was shooting at him from a feed barn that stood at a forty-five degree angle to his left, Vejar used the horse as a shield while he hastily untied the reins from the rail.

But Ben came up from behind the trough to open up at him with his handgun. A single shot in reply from Vejar and the huge Poole brother took cover quickly. Swinging the horse around, Vejar mounted on the side away from Lew Poole. Keeping low in the saddle, bent forward on the stirrups, he set off at a gallop with reins at the right tension.

Ben Poole loomed up in front of him, confident that he could bide his time and pick off Vejar easily from close range. A rifle bullet from his brother changed his mind. Passing close to Vejar, the bullet continued on its way to whip the Stetson off Ben's head. A startled Ben dropped rapidly back under cover.

Unable to believe his good fortune, Vejar spurred the horse. He had passed Ben and the house and was within a few yards of being out of the range of Lew Poole's rifle, when the horse gave what sounded like a cross between a deep cough and a low scream. Its pace faltered, but only momentarily. Relieved as his mount recovered its gallop, Vejar was shocked as the horse suddenly folded underneath him.

Catapulted over the animal's head, he sailed through the air, just managing to tuck his head into his shoulders before he hit the ground with an impact that jarred every bone in his body.

*

Looking out on to the street in the hope of catching sight of the still absent Fallon Vejar, Raya was surprised to see Carmel dismounting outside of the church, and reaching to pull her rifle from its scabbard. Raya opened the door and called to her, 'Come in quickly, Carmel. You won't need a rifle. We are just women and children in here.'

'What's happening?' Carmel asked, as she hurried into the church, bringing her rifle with her despite what Raya had said. They were in the foyer, from where the door into the main part of the church was open and the chattering gathering of women and children could be both seen and heard.

'You've arrived at the wrong time, Carmel,' Raya said worriedly. 'A little later and you could have been in real danger out on the street. A gang of bank robbers is heading into town right now.'

'Really,' Carmel exclaimed mildly, puzzling Raya with her coolness in so dire a situation. Then she enquired conversationally. 'Is your friend here, Raya?'

'Mary? She's in the church.'

'Would you mind asking her to come here?' Carmel enquired.

'Of course,' a mystified Raya said, as she went off into the church.

When she returned with Mary Alcott at her side, Carmel greeted the other girl with a quick smile, then nodded at the door Raya had left open. 'Please close that door, Raya.'

Obeying, a frowning Raya came back to question Carmel. 'I don't understand, Carmel.'

'I'm sorry, Raya, but my name is not Carmel Morrow.'

'Then what should I call you?' a bewildered Raya asked.

'If you want to call me anything after I've said what I have to say,' answered the woman, who in the past few minutes had turned into a somehow frightening stranger to Raya, 'Gloria will do. Please believe me when I say that I really enjoyed our short friendship, Raya. I am one of the outlaw band about to rob the bank here at Yancey. Until my friends are ready to leave town, I have to hold you and Mary here as hostages.'

Understanding came suddenly to Raya. 'It's Fallon Vejar, isn't it? You believe that Fallon won't take any action while you are holding me.'

'I am sure that he won't risk you being harmed, Raya.'

'But why Mary?' Raya noticed that Gloria's dark complexion had paled at this question. That made her terribly afraid for Mary.

Turning to walk away to the door of the church, Gloria didn't answer. Pushing the door ajar, she swiftly beckoned Raya to her side and asked, 'Who is that important looking *hombre* going into that place where you and me had tea?'

'That's Walter Randall, Yancey's mayor.'

'Go back over and stand where you were,' Gloria ordered.

Raya meekly did as she was told.

With their horses at walking pace, they rode into town three abreast. Klugg was in the middle, and he and his two outlaw companions were vigilant. Their eyes continually flicked from left to right, checking out the buildings on either side of them as they moved up the street.

'Quiet,' Mitchell Staley remarked unnecessarily.

'Don't let that fool you,' the mulatto advised.

'Quit talking and keep watching,' Ken Klugg snapped at them. Then he relaxed a little and pointed up the street. 'Everything's real purty, boys. There's Gloria up at the church door.'

Continuing at the same steady rate, they reached the church where Gloria Malone now stood waiting inside the partly open door.

'You have the girl, Gloria?'

'Yes, she and the other girl are here with me.'

'Vejar?' Klugg asked in a tight voice.

'I haven't seen him,' Gloria said. She nodded her head at the Chinese teashop across the street. 'The town's head *honcho* is in that place. His name is Randall.'

Without another word, Klugg pulled on the reins and headed across the street. His two gang members followed loyally. When Klugg dismounted, so did they. All three stepped up on to the boardwalk together. As Klugg drew his Colt from its holster in preparation for entering the teashop, Jack and Staley took up positions, one each side of the door. Rifles held obliquely at the ready in front of them, they kept watch.

The gang leader opened the door, stepped inside, closed the door behind him and waited for a moment, listening. Hearing a low murmur of voices coming from behind a closed door, he walked over stealthily. Pulling back his right leg, he kicked the door open so violently that it shattered. Framed in the doorway, he covered those in the room with the gun held at his hip. A Chinese man and a woman stood nearest to him, alarm on their faces. Looking shocked at the dramatic entrance were four men who were standing round a bed. A man lay propped up on the bed, his upper body swathed in bandages.

'Ken Klugg,' the injured man weakly identified the intruder.

Ignoring this, Klugg asked, 'Where's Vejar?'

When no answer was forthcoming, Klugg grinned and said, 'That's the way Vejar likes to play his hand.' Then he glared at the four men before asking, 'Which one of you is Randall?'

'I am Walter Randall,' responded a man with a hawked-nosed, lean face and a body that had run to fat. He struck an arrogant pose with both thumbs hooked into the small pockets of his vest.

'Well hear me, Randall, and hear me real good,' Klugg said. 'Tell Vejar we're holding Raya Kennedy over at the church—'

'Good God!' Randall exclaimed as realization hit him. 'That woman we sent to the church.'

'I do the talking, Randall, and you do the listening,' Klugg said menacingly. 'Tell Vejar what I'm telling you. Our business in your town will be over quickly unless someone tries to interfere. If that happens, then the girl will die. That's a promise, Randall. But I don't hold with unnecessary killing, so let Vejar know that he can find me waiting for him outside the church. Tell him that we can do a deal so that nobody gets hurt.' He walked over to the bed and looked down at the man on it. 'I guess that you're George Harker.'

'You guess right.'

'Hopefully we'll meet again one day, when you

are well enough to strap on your gun.'

'I'd like that, Klugg,' Harker agreed, his voice fading from weakness. 'But I sure as hell believe that Fallon Vejar will rob me of that pleasure.'

Dismissing this with a derisive, mirthless chuckle, Klugg brought his attention back to Randall. 'I'm leaving you all now, but be warned, Randall. If any one of you as much as pokes his nose out into the street, then he will die where he stands.'

'No one will give you any trouble if you will just release the girl,' Randall pleaded.

'You ain't in no position to bargain, Randall,' Klugg snarled. 'Remember, you and Vejar have been warned.'

With that, Klugg backed out of the room. Silence prevailed until the street door closed noisily behind him.

Badly shaken, Vejar lay on his side where he had hit the ground. Close to him he heard the last breath leave the horse in a prolonged gasp. With the spinning in his head slowing so that he was able to grasp something of what was going on around him, he saw Ben Poole approaching him slowly and cautiously, a six-gun aimed at him unwaveringly.

Reaching under himself, Vejar discovered thankfully that his own .45 had not been jolted from its holster when he had been thrown from the horse. Keeping his movements to a minimum, he drew the gun and tucked it in close to his chest. Then he played dead, hoping the moronic Ben would lack the good sense to put a bullet in him before coming too close.

'Vejar?' Ben had stopped to call questioningly.

Lying absolutely still, Vejar continued to feign what could be construed either as unconsciousness or death. It was a perilous ploy. Should Ben Poole decide it was the former, then he would put a bullet into Vejar before taking a risk in coming closer. Even if undecided as to Vejar's state, it would be logical to take the same precaution.

But Ben was a thug, not a thinker. Waiting a little while longer for a response from Vejar, he came on to stand over him. Hearing the click as Poole thumbed back the hammer of his Colt, Vejar knew the time had come. Opening his eyes, he fired from where he held his .45 in close to his body. With Vejar deprived of the opportunity to take aim, his bullet hit Poole in the stomach. Going backwards for some distance without his feet touching the ground, Ben crashed down onto his back, shrieking loudly as the sheer agony of a stomach wound kicked in. His six-gun flew out of his hand, firing a shot harmlessly when it hit the ground.

Knowing that Lew Poole would have by now moved in closer, Vejar sprang up and ran to crouch behind a water butt. The injured Ben was writhing on the floor, bending and straightening his legs in a vain attempt at easing the excruciating pain of his wound. His screaming was harrowing to hear, and Vejar felt sorry for the stricken man.

A flurry of movement caught his eye as Lew Poole ran towards cover provided by a corner of the house. Vejar had no time to get off a shot. Ben's horrific screaming went on. In between screams, he cried out, 'Help me, Lew. Please help stop the pain.'

There was no response from Lew Poole, and the injured man's screams continued to rip through the air. The need to ride into Yancey had Vejar racking his brain to come up with a way of breaking the deadlock. The principal factor against him was that Lew had a rifle. Were it simply an equal contest limited to sidearms, then it would be easier for him to find a solution.

Lew Poole called his name. 'Vejar.'

'Yes?'

'We have to help Ben.'

'*You* have to help Ben,' Vejar replied. 'He's your brother, Lew.'

Ben's distress had become even more disturbing now, and he was sobbing as he cried out for someone to help him.

His brother shouted, 'In the name of all that's holy, Vejar, we can't leave a man to suffer in this way. Where is Michael?'

'In the house, dead,' Vejar answered bluntly.

A prolonged silence followed. When Lew Poole called out again it was in a conciliatory tone. 'Listen to me, Vejar. What was between you and me is finished as far as I'm concerned. I've lost one brother today, and I don't want to lose another.'

'What do you suggest, Lew?' Vejar enquired.

'You holster your gun and I'll throw out my rifle. We'll do what we can for Ben, and then you'll be free to ride out of here. I'm speaking the truth, Vejar. Here's my rifle.' Lew's arm came out from behind the house to toss his rifle into the dust. 'Now I'll count to three and we'll both step out with our hands up. I can't say fairer than that.'

Turning the proposition over in his mind, Vejar reminded himself that only a fool would trust a Poole. But the situation was an extraordinary one. He found Ben's screaming difficult to bear. It was highly unlikely that Lew would try to double-cross him, as the eldest Poole brother could never beat him on the draw. The pressing situation in Yancey was the deciding factor in

Vejar calling out that he agreed.

'One ... two ... three ...' Lew Poole counted.

They both stepped out, guns holstered and hands above their heads. Vejar said, 'Lower your hands, Lew, and we'll do what we can for your brother.'

When they got to Ben, both of them knew that he was beyond help. The screaming had ebbed to become a low groaning, and the huge body was convulsing. Looking up at the older brother, Vejar advised, 'All you can do for Ben is say *adios*, Lew.'

Close to tears, Lew nodded. But then the unexpected happened. Ben Poole opened eyes that, though glazing over, were filled with hatred for Vejar. Amazingly for a man on the edge of death, Ben flung out a massive arm to grab Vejar by the ankle. Trying to free himself and remain upright, Vejar was aware that Lew Poole was going for his gun.

Drawing his own .45, Vejar fired and Lew dropped with a bullet hole between his eyes, his own gun unfired. To get his leg free, Vejar was ready to shoot Ben. But then the thick fingers holding his ankle relaxed, the heavy arm fell away from him. With nothing more than a slight rattling in his throat, Ben Poole died.

Holstering his gun, Vejar sprinted to where

Ben's horse stood docilely with its head down. Vaulting up over the rear of the horse into the saddle, he reached for the reins to pull the horse round hard and set off at a gallop along the beaten track that led to Yancey.

NINE

With those around him protesting, George Harker struggled to sit upright on the bed and swing round to place both feet on the floor. In obvious pain and with his forehead beaded with sweat, he reached for his clothes. Refusing help, it took him a long time to get dressed. His first attempt at getting to his feet was a disaster. Randall rushed to his aid.

'Leave me, Walter,' Harker ordered, as he sat back down heavily on the bed.

'You are his doctor, John,' Randall pleaded with Thurston. 'You must put a stop to this.'

With a negative shake of his head, Thurston explained, 'The sheriff is simply a patient I am treating for a gunshot wound, Walter, nothing more than that. I would not take it upon myself to tell a man what or what not to do.'

'What I have to do is go across to the church to help Raya,' Harker said resolutely.

'We can't permit you to even try such a thing,' Henry Drake protested.

'You had better not try to stop me, Henry,' Harker warned. His eyes scanned the room. Then he said, 'Pass me that broom, Wu.'

Obediently, the Chinaman fetched the soft sweeping brush with a long handle that Harker had pointed at. He passed it to the sheriff, who turned it upside down and placed the head under his left armpit. Using the broom as a crutch, Harker eased himself upright off the bed and stood for a moment to allow his sense of balance to settle. Next, still supported by the broom but with both hands free, he picked up his gunbelt and buckled it on.

His clumsy first attempt at drawing his six-gun was a failure that made Walter Randall complain, 'This is madness, George. Give it up.'

Ignoring this advice, Harker rehearsed his draw again and again. At last his gun was clearing leather, but in comparison to his old skill it lacked both co-ordination and speed. Without a word, Lin Chua walked to a dresser that held Harker's clean bandages and medication. She took out a bottle of whiskey and a tumbler, filling it to the rim. Crossing the room in her soft-footed way, she passed the full glass to Harker.

Raising the glass to his mouth, Harker drank deeply. Pausing for a moment to let the liquor work its magic, he then drained the glass.

Looking much stronger now, he reached for his gun. This time it was a fast draw, but the men present were only too well aware that what they had witnessed was a shadow of Harker's former expertise.

Holstering his gun, the sheriff made his way to the street door. Seeing how dependent Harker was on the support of the broom, Henry Drake made a final plea. 'Don't do it, George. I am certain that Vejar is out there somewhere, and he will deal with this.'

Neither replying nor taking a backward glance, Harker, clinging to the handle of the broom with his left hand, opened the door with his right hand and stepped out into the street.

Afraid for Mary more than she was for herself, Raya asked, 'What is going to happen to us, Carmel?'

'My name isn't Carmel.'

'Sorry. Gloria.'

Raya had made the name mistake because although the outlaw woman tried to assume a tough, threatening manner, the nice person that Raya had known, albeit briefly, could easily be detected below the surface. Since two of the townwomen had some time ago opened the church door to enquire what was happening in the hall, and Gloria had shouted at them to go back in and shut the door, the three of them had been alone.

'What is going to happen to us?' Raya tried enquiring once more.

'I don't want anything to happen to either of you, Raya,' Gloria confessed.

Indicating the rifle that the outlaw held in the crook of her right arm, Raya asked, 'Then why are you holding us captive?'

Taking some Bull Durham and papers from her shirt pocket, Gloria didn't respond while she deftly rolled a cigarette. Putting the cigarette in her mouth she flicked a match with a thumbnail to ignite it. Lighting the cigarette, she inhaled deeply, held her breath, and then exhaled a smoky sigh.

'Your lifestyle and mine are very different, Raya,' she explained quietly. 'I am an outlaw, and therefore have to rob in order to eat, to live. Unfortunately, you and your friend are a part of our plan to rob the bank, and I am under orders.'

'Orders to do what?' Raya enquired fearfully, but if Gloria had intended to reply, a fist hammering on the door prevented her from doing so.

'Are you all ready in there if I need you, Gloria?' a man's voice shouted.

'I'm ready,' Gloria called back, then asked with a little tremor in her voice. 'Has Fallon Vejar shown up?'

Raya joined Gloria in a suspenseful wait for an answer.

'No,' the male voice shouted. 'But what I'd say is Sheriff George Harker has just come out on the street and is heading my way. He's using a stick to limp along, so he isn't likely to cause me any bother. But you be ready just in case he does-n't see sense.'

Glancing at Raya and Mary, sadness in her eyes, Gloria brought her rifle round in front of her and held it with both hands. Then she called to the man outside. 'I'll be ready.'

Intimidated by Gloria's stance with her rifle, Raya and Mary reached for and clasped each other's hands tightly.

Having got down off the boardwalk into the street with difficulty, George Harker started slowly and painfully across the street. Klugg stood outside the church, his jacket pulled back clear of his holstered gun. Another outlaw stood beside him in the deceptively relaxed stance of a mountain lion about to spring on its prey. The experienced Harker spotted a mulatto who stood holding a rifle up on the flat roof of a building next to the church. The odds were stacked against him, but Harker was undeterred.

'Hold it right there, Sheriff,' Klugg said, when Harker was in the centre of the street. 'Where's Vejar?'

'He'll be here, Klugg. But right now this is between you and me,' Harker replied, swaying a little as the effort in crossing the street sapped his already depleted strength.

Seeing this brought a grin to Klugg's face. He shifted his hips a little, ready for action, then said quietly, 'Then I guess you'd better slap leather, Sheriff.'

'This is bad.'

A grim-faced Walter Randall gave his muttered opinion as he and the others watched from the teashop window. There could be only one ending to what was happening in the street, and it horrified them to think of it. Though unable to hear what was being said, it was plain that the outlaw leader was taunting the courageous sheriff.

Dr Thurston warned them hoarsely, 'George Harker is on the verge of collapse.'

'A thousand curses on Vejar for getting us into this position,' Henry Drake moaned.

'*Us?*' Thurston questioned cynically. 'It's the sheriff who's in this position, not us, Henry.'

'No,' Randall said loudly and resolutely. 'No,

goddammit, it's time we gave Harker some help.'

Going to the back of the room, he picked up a shotgun and hurried back to the window. The Chinese couple released an involuntarily duet of squealing as Randall used the butt of the weapon to shatter the windowpane. The doctor and Henry Drake first protested loudly, then begged Randall not to use the gun. Unheeding, he rested the barrel of the shotgun on the bottom of the now glassless window frame and pointed it across the street.

Everything happened fast from that moment on. Too fast for anyone to take it all in. His damaged body letting him down at last, Sheriff George Harker crumpled on to the dusty street and lay inert. Klugg and the outlaw beside him dropped to the boardwalk and lay flat. With the muzzle of the shotgun menacing them through the broken window across the street, Klugg yelled, 'Whoever you are, lay down that weapon or face the consequences.'

Henry Drake pleaded with Randall. 'You have to do what he says, Walter.'

'Put the gun down, Walter,' Dr Thurston ordered, but was ignored by Randall.

Still lying flat, Klugg shot his right leg back to kick the door of the church, calling out, 'Do it, *now*!'

The hysterical screaming of a woman quickly followed the sharp bark of a rifle inside the church. The screaming continued, becoming unearthly as it spiralled higher. It seemed to gain volume in the teashop as it echoed around the room. The white-faced occupants looked at each other in dismay.

Letting go of the shotgun as he slumped into a sitting position on the floor, Walter Randall groaned, 'What have I done?'

'You've got young Raya Kennedy shot,' Henry Drake told him accusingly.

John Thurston silenced them as Klugg started to shout from across the street. 'You there. If you stay out of this, then nobody else will get hurt.'

'I'm a doctor,' Thurston called back. 'The sheriff will die if he's left lying out there. Will you allow us to bring him in?'

'No. The sheriff got himself where he is, so he'll have to make his own way back,' Klugg answered coldly. Then he asked, 'Where's Vejar?'

'That's what we'd like to know,' Dr Thurston whispered to no one in particular.

At last succeeding in calming down the distraught Mary Alcott, Raya wiped her friend's eyes and face with a handkerchief. A sobbing Mary croaked, 'I thought I was about to die.'

Raya looked gratefully at Gloria, who had deliberately fired her rifle into the floor. Sensing Raya's eyes on her, Gloria kept her head turned away as she said, 'Don't ride your luck, either of you. That's probably the last chance I'll have to do either of you a favour.'

'There was no shooting outside, so I hope that George is all right,' Raya mused anxiously.

'I doubt it,' Gloria warned, 'and things are sure to get worse.' She added worriedly, 'It would have gone without a hitch had Vejar been here. Do you know where he is, Raya?'

Raya shook her head. 'I don't. I can't understand it, because Fallon wouldn't let George Harker down.'

'Fallon isn't the type to let anyone down,' Gloria commented softly.

'Do you know him?' an astonished Raya enquired, surprised to experience a painful stab of jealousy.

'I know him,' Gloria replied.

Then she said no more.

Dismounting at the edge of town when he heard the rifle shot, Vejar continued up the deserted street on foot, keeping in tight to the buildings. There was no sign of any activity at the bank just up ahead. That supported Vejar's estimation that the sound of the shot had come from further up the street. Guessing that Walter Randall had put the two lads in position inside the bank, he bent over double to avoid being blasted by shotgun pellets as he passed the window.

To his left, four horses were hitched to a rail close to the church. Recognizing Gloria Malone's palomino, he knew that the Klugg gang was in town.

On noticing something odd about the appearance of Wu Chua's teashop, Vejar backed into a doorway while he studied the place. The movement of a cloud across the sun solved the problem for him by revealing a broken window. Moving out from the doorway, Vejar spotted the figure of a man lying face downwards in the street. Unable to identify the prone figure, he accepted that the danger lay in the vicinity of the Chinese man's place. His guess was that Randall and the other town councillors had moved into the teashop to be with George Harker when the bank robbers had arrived. There wasn't a fighting man among them, except for the sheriff, whose gunshot wound had put him out of action. That made the shattered window all the more perturbing.

Needing to find out the exact situation as soon as possible, he ran across the street. Turning into an alleyway, he made his way to the back of Wu Chua's premises. Reaching the high fence of the back yard, he stretched his arms upward to grasp the top of the wooden fence, and pulled himself up.

'The town's wide open,' a pleased Klugg commented to Mitchell Staley. 'The sheriff's lying over there in the dust. Vejar isn't going to show now. He has abandoned his own people, and those old-timers across the street won't cause us no more bother.'

'So we move on the bank now?' Staley, who had been growing impatient at the delay, said hopefully.

'I'll get Jack down from the roof and we'll go—' Klugg shut off in mid-sentence as the mulatto shouted down from his rooftop position.

'Klugg,' Jack yelled. 'Vejar's just climbed over the back fence of that place across the street.'

Tanned face instantly losing its pleased expression, Klugg called back 'Are you sure, Jack?'

'I'm sure.'

'I guess this changes everything,' Mitchell Staley said. Though made fearless by the harsh life he had led, he found himself longing right then to be anywhere other than in the town of Yancey.

Vejar's jaw muscles clenched as he listened to the three councillors. Desperately worried at hearing that Klugg held Raya hostage, he was badly shaken when John Thurston added that they had good reason to believe that she had already been killed.

'You can't be certain of that,' Vejar argued, in an attempt at giving himself hope.

'There was a shot and a woman screamed,' Henry Drake explained.

'So, what are we to do, Vejar?' enquired Walter Randall, having largely recovered from his distress at causing what was probably a fatal incident. 'Klugg and one of his men are over there outside of the church, and there's another man with a rifle up on Mortimer's flat roof.'

That meant it was Gloria Malone inside the church. Hopeful for a moment that the opportunity might present itself for him to talk to Gloria, Vejar dismissed the idea. She was an outlaw robbing a bank, and would not be dissuaded from her purpose.

He answered Randall. 'The first thing is to get George in off the street to see if there's anything the doc can do for him. Henry, will you come out with Walter to carry the sheriff back in?'

Swallowing hard, Henry Drake said, 'Of

course I will, but aren't we likely to be gunned down once we step out of the door?'

Not replying, Vejar went to the window. Keeping to one side, he called out. 'Klugg, this is Fallon Vejar.'

'So, you showed up at last,' Klugg shouted back.

'I'm coming out, Ken, and bringing two men with me to take Sheriff Harker back inside.'

'Seeing that it's you, Fallon, I'll agree to that. But none of your tricks. Your *compadres* have already forced me to have one hostage shot. It won't bother me none if you make it so's we have to shoot the second one. The way I hear it as far as you're concerned, we've kept the important one until last.'

Learning that Raya was still alive was cold comfort for Vejar in this situation. Any attempt to thwart Klugg's determination to rob the bank would result in him killing Raya without a second thought.

'We're coming out,' he told Klugg.

'Then you keep your hands on your head at all times, Vejar.'

Doing as Klugg had ordered, Vejar came out of the teashop with Randall and Drake following behind him nervously. Thurston overtook all three of them to reach George Harker and kneel down beside him. After a swift examination, the doctor called to Vejar and the others. 'He's alive, but we need to get him inside.'

'Pick him up,' Vejar told Randall and Drake.

Struggling with the weight of the heavily built sheriff, the two councillors got him off the ground and Vejar followed as they headed back to the teashop. He halted and slowly turned when Klugg called his name.

'Vejar.'

Silently waiting, Vejar stared coldly at Klugg.

'I'll tell you how it's going to be, Fallon,' Klugg began. 'We came into town to hit the bank, and that's what we're going to do. You go on back inside. There must be no interference, or that girl in there will die. You understand?'

'I understand,' Vejar conceded. 'I won't risk the girl's life. But there are two boys armed with shotguns inside the bank. They don't deserve to die, Ken.'

'Then they shouldn't have volunteered,' Klugg replied unfeelingly.

Lowering his hands to his sides, Vejar said, 'Then you and me better settle it here and now.'

'Put your hands back on your head,' an apprehensive Klugg shouted.

Ignoring the order, Vejar's right hand hovered above the handle of his holstered gun. He said calmly, 'This is showdown time, Ken. Either you let me get those two lads safely out of the bank, or you make your play right here and now.'

'You don't stand a chance, Fallon. If you get lucky and beat me to the draw, Mitch and Jack will fill you with lead.'

'That's not your way,' Vejar said, shaking his head. 'You're too proud a man for that to happen, Ken.'

Spreading both hands wide, palms up, in a gesture of resignation, Klugg said, 'I guess you're right. Anyway, I'd prefer not to face a couple of scatterguns. Go back inside and leave your gun, then I'll go with you while you talk those two kids into giving up their weapons.'

TEN

Cautiously staying back and to one side of the bank's door, Vejar called, 'This is Fallon Vejar. Can you hear me, Jonathan?'

With Klugg beside him, Vejar waited for a response. Mitchell Staley and Jack the mulatto had remained outside the church. The empty street had a tense and menacing atmosphere. The three councillors had been against Vejar's plan for the two lads to give up their shotguns, seeing it as abject surrender to the outlaws. But a rapidly recovering George Harker had agreed with Vejar. They could no more gamble with the lives of the two boys than they could risk Raya's life.

Urged by an impatient Klugg, Vejar called once more, 'Jonathan.'

'I can hear you.'

'I want you and Len to open the door just far

145

enough to throw out your shotguns.'

'Why should we do that?' Jonathan enquired in a quavering voice.

'Because that's what I want you to do.'

'How do I know that you are who you say you are?'

Then Hiram Anstey's voice came from inside of the bank. 'I recognize your voice, Vejar, but I won't leave my bank undefended.'

'No amount of money is worth the lives of those young lads, Hiram,' Vejar called.

'While they have their guns we still have a chance,' Anstey argued.

Exasperated by the delay, Klugg beckoned to Staley and Jack. The two outlaws came hurrying down the street as Vejar tried to negotiate with Jonathan instead of Anstey.

'Jonathan, you and Len will both die very soon if you hold on to your weapons.'

No immediate answer was forthcoming, but then Jonathan said, 'Mr Anstey says that Uncle Walter would want me to keep the gun and help save the bank.'

'What's happening now?' Henry Drake asked anxiously.

At the window, Sheriff George Harker reported, 'The two outlaws who were standing across the street have moved off to the bank.

That gives me the chance to go over to the church.'

'Vejar will have a free hand without Raya to worry about,' Harker said, as he stepped out of the door.

He planned to go in the door at the rear of the church and surprise the woman outlaw who, according to Vejar, was an expert with a gun. But he would need to be careful not to put Raya or anyone else in more danger.

Reaching the side of the church, he made his way down to the rear of the building. Inside, he raised a hand for quiet. The threat of violence seemed to have awoken something primitive in the crowd of females. He asked them to stay calm. Making his way to the door into the hall, Harker didn't risk turning the handle. Drawing his gun he kicked the door open.

Stepping awkwardly into the room, the sheriff's experienced eye instantly took in the situation. A frightened Raya and Mary Alcott stood to one side. In front of him was a black-haired, dark woman who held a rifle pointed at him. Intent on protecting Raya and Mary, Harker brought his gun to bear on the beautiful outlaw.

He was squeezing the trigger when the unexpected happened. Suddenly lashing out, Raya hit his gun arm. The impact caused Harker to lose his balance. The broom handle slid sideways on the polished floor, and his gun fell from his hand as he toppled sideways. Hitting the floor in an embarrassing sitting position, the sheriff looked up into the dark muzzle of a rifle and the sardonic smile of the female outlaw.

Vejar was agonizingly aware that he had no gun, and any plan he might come up with would be impractical because Raya was held hostage. He asked Klugg, 'Give me a few minutes to talk to Anstey. How else are you going to get into the bank? You'd need dynamite to blow that heavy door off its hinges.'

With a cynical chuckle, Klugg said, 'All that interests that *hombre* is money.' He added grudgingly, 'Go ahead then, Fallon.'

It was ironic that Anstey had as much a hunger for money as Klugg had, yet Vejar believed that deep down Hiram was a decent man. Though the banker regarded the boys with shotguns as a safeguard against his bank being robbed, it wasn't likely that he could bear the thought of a girl being shot in cold blood because of the stance that he was taking.

'I'm coming up to the door alone, Hiram,' Vejar called in warning.

'You won't make me change my mind,' Anstey's voice said defiantly.

'I think that I will,' Vejar said. 'They are holding Raya Kennedy captive, Hiram. If we don't go along with them they will shoot her. They've already killed one girl hostage.'

'Was that the shot that I heard earlier?' Anstey enquired querulously.

'Yes. The best thing you can do is open this door, Hiram.'

'Which will mean my bank being robbed,' Anstey complained.

'I give you my word that I will do everything in my power to get your money back,' Vejar pledged.

After what to Vejar seemed an eternity, Anstey said despondently, 'I'll take your word on that, Vejar. Now stand back.'

Vejar took a few steps backwards as he heard the bank door first being unbolted and then unlocked. Coming up behind him in his lithe, cat-like way of moving, Klugg waited with Vejar. The door opened a little and in his urgency to enter the bank, Klugg was passing Vejar when the blast of a shotgun came from inside. Reeling back, the right side of his face peppered with shot and beginning to bleed, Klugg prepared to fire into the bank through the gap in the door.

Overwhelmed by fear for the two boys and Anstey inside, Vejar momentarily forgot Raya's perilous situation, and leapt at Klugg. He had one arm around the outlaw-leader's neck, when Jack came from behind to smash him hard over the head with the barrel of a Peacemaker.

Collapsing as unbearable pain filled his head, Vejar heard another blast from a shotgun as he fell unconscious to the boardwalk.

'I'm so sorry, George.'

Harker heard Raya's whispered apology as, with as much dignity as possible, he clambered up from the floor. Feeling weakness threatening to overcome him yet again, he was in a cold sweat. But he held the outlaw woman's dark-eyed gaze, defying her to fire the rifle. An awed Raya and Mary held their breath as the sheriff stood waiting fearlessly.

A sudden movement by Gloria Malone brought gasps from the other two girls. In a practised, fluid movement, Gloria let her right arm drop, using a flip of her hand to twirl the rifle, then caught it so that the butt and not the muzzle pointed at Harker.

Holding out the weapon to him, she said, 'I guess my heart is no longer in this, Sheriff.'

'Then you are under arrest, ma'am,' Harker said, as he took the rifle from her.

Gloria gave a reverse shrug, a slumping of shoulders that signalled her indifference.

*

Turning away from the teashop window, disbelief registered on his ruddy features, Henry Drake announced to the others, 'Dang me if Harker isn't coming back with Raya, Mary Alcott, and what I assume is the woman desperado.'

The others clustered around him excitedly to watch the man and three women cross the street. They greeted Harker and the two Yancey women as they came in through the door. Face pale from exertion, the sheriff passed the rifle to Randall and pointed to Gloria Malone, saying. 'Keep her under guard at all times, Walter. When things are right out there I'll take her down to the jail and lock her in a cell.'

'There's been some shooting at the bank, George,' Dr Thurston said, helping the exhausted sheriff into a chair.

'I heard it,' Harker answered. 'But I'm not up to doing anything about it right now.'

Henry Drake complimented him. 'You've done plenty, George.'

Vejar regained consciousness to find the mulatto outlaw lying dead in the street beside him. The huge area of Jack's chest that was bloodied told Vejar that he had died from a shotgun wound. Everything around him was still and quiet. The door of the bank was open. Raising himself up on to his knees, Vejar lowered his head to send a rush of blood to aid his spinning brain.

After a minute or so in this position, he got up and made his unsteady way into the bank. An ashen-faced Hiram Anstey sat slumped in a chair behind his huge desk. Eyes staring fixedly, the banker was speechless, pointing with a shaking hand at a safe that was open and empty.

The lad named Len was sprawled on the floor with his upper back against a wall. A cursory glance told Vejar the boy was dead. Jonathan was lying face down across the teller's desk. Turning him over gently, Vejar saw blood pumping thickly from a stomach wound. Laying the boy carefully on the floor, Vejar ripped a hand towel from a hook on the wall, folded it into a pad and pressed it against Jonathan's wound to staunch the bleeding.

'Hiram,' he shouted. 'Get hold of yourself and come over here.'

It took three more angry shouts from Vejar before the banker came over shakily to look at the bloody pad in distaste before Vejar could get him to hold it in place. Then Vejar looked around the bank for a weapon, but Klugg and Staley had taken the shotguns as well as the money.

'I'll send Doc Thurston along as soon as possible,' Vejar told Anstey.

Going out of the bank, he turned down an

alleyway that took him to the rear of the buildings, aware that another passageway would bring him out to where the outlaws' horses were hitched. Vejar hurried, desperately wanting to find Klugg, Staley and Gloria before they could leave town. Though he was unarmed, he accepted that this was a time for action.

Nearing the end of the passage, he saw the outlaws' four horses still hitched. Mitchell Staley stood packing bulging moneybags into the saddle-bags. Neither Klugg nor Gloria was anywhere in sight. Moving silently, Vejar came within a few feet away from Staley. The outlaw was so intent on his task that he was oblivious to Vejar's presence.

Vejar was taking a few more steps, when Staley sensed someone behind him and turned. Vegar's left hand grabbed and held Staley's wrist in a vice-like grip, while using the edge of his right hand to deliver a powerful blow to the throat. Eyes protruding so that it seemed they would burst from their sockets, Staley coughed repeatedly until the coughing changed into a wheezing, choking sound. A pitiless Vejar kneed his adversary in the groin. Stepping back as Staley began to fall, Vejar lashed out with his right foot. His boot caught the collapsing Staley full in the face with such force that it sent the outlaw's head back, snapping his neck. The sharp crack of the breaking vertebrae was resounding in the street when the louder reporter of a six-shooter drowned it out.

A bullet that missed Vejar by less than an inch, entered the head of the horse nearest to him. Shrieking out in pain and panic, the horse reared up on its hind legs, flaying the air with its front hoofs. The diversion gave Vejar the opportunity to snatch the dead Staley's gun from its holster. The horse fell with its head suspended from the hitching rail by reins that had twisted around its neck. One of its eyes was just a black hole that slowly wept blood, while the remaining eye stared accusingly at Vejar as the animal breathed its last.

Vejar forced his attention back on whoever had fired at him. The street was deserted. Klugg had to be in hiding, standing guard over Staley while he stashed the stolen money away. He had been unable to fire at Vejar without the danger of hitting Staley.

Uncertainty about Raya's safety deterred Vejar from searching for Klugg. Holding Staley's .45, Vejar moved into the street waiting for Klugg to show himself. But the outlaw leader stayed hidden as an alert Vejar made his way to the teashop. Astonished to see both Raya and Gloria there, Vejar was embarrassed when Raya impulsively rushed forward to hug him in full view of George Harker. But Harker shook him by the hand while

Henry Drake explained how the sheriff had rescued Raya and captured the female outlaw.

Vejar told them, 'Either Jonathan or Len got the mulatto with a shotgun.'

'Are the boys safe and well?' Randall anxiously enquired.

'I'm sorry, Randall,' Vejar replied. 'Len is dead, and Jonathan badly hurt.' He turned to Thurston. 'You'll be at risk, Doc, but will you come to the bank with me?'

Replying without hesitation, Thurston said, 'I'll fetch my bag.'

'I'll take John down to the bank. You are needed here, Fallon.' Harker said.

'No.' Gloria unexpectedly spoke up. 'You are in no shape to deal with Klugg, Sheriff. He's as quick and as deadly as a riled rattler.'

'Whose side are you really on, Gloria?' Raya asked wonderingly.

'Right now I'm not sure,' Gloria answered with a self-deprecating grin.

'Gloria spoke the truth, George. You look after things here,' Vejar said, picking up his own gun, spinning the chamber before holstering it. 'The women must stay in the church.'

'Until it's over,' Harker agreed. 'I'll stay by the window with my rifle and pick Klugg off if he tries to collect the horses and saddle-bags across the street.'

'Don't underestimate Klugg, George, he's clever,' Vejar advised, as Thurston returned with his bag.

'Take great care,' Raya called after Vejar, as he and the doctor went out of the door.

When the door had closed behind the pair, Raya walked over to join the sheriff at the window. She enquired, 'I am sorry about what I did in the church, George, but Gloria wouldn't harm us.'

'Don't worry about that.' Harker's eyes took on a distant look as he said. 'Raya?'

'Yes?'

'Fallon Vejar coming back has kind of changed things, hasn't it?'

Deliberately misconstruing what he'd said, Raya said, 'Yancey certainly hasn't known another day like today.'

'What I'm saying, Raya,' Harker went on, 'is that I won't hold you to anything.'

Keenly aware of her own muddled feelings about Vejar, Raya was saved from further talk on the subject as Klugg boldly emerged from the passageway beside the church. Startled, Harker was raising his rifle when Gloria spoke from the centre of the room.

'Lower your rifle, Sheriff.'

Raya saw that Gloria had picked up the dead outlaw's .45 that Vejar had left on a table, and was aiming it at Harker. Randall, Drake and the Chuas watched in shocked helplessness.

'What are you doing, Gloria?' Raya gasped.

'I won't see Ken Klugg shot down in the street like a dog,' Gloria answered.

Lowering his rifle, Harker used a movement of his eyes to have Raya look to her left out of the window. Her heart missed a beat as she saw Vejar and Dr Thurston heading their way.

A feeling that was a blend of expectation and apprehension had been growing stronger in Vejar on his way along the street, reaching a peak as the teashop neared. His reflexes came instantly into play when he heard Harker's voice shout a warning.

'Fallon. Klugg is in the mouth of the alley beside the church.'

'Get into Chua's place fast, Doc,' he ordered, Thurston who had removed a bullet from Jonathan, whom they had left at the bank.

Halting, Vejar turned to face the passageway and Ken Klugg. The right side of his face was swollen and as red as raw meat. Taking a step forward, Klugg said, 'This hasn't been a good day, Fallon.'

'Not for you, Ken,' Vejar agreed. 'I guess you've lost.'

Shaking his head, Klugg said, 'No, that's what

is bothering me. There is no winner or loser here, and that just ain't right.'

'What are you saying, Ken?' Vejar asked, as they shortened the distance between them. 'It's simple, Fallon. There's my money there, packed on my horses. The problem is that I can't take it because you will stop me, and I can't let you stop me.'

'So, this is a showdown between you and me?'

'That's what I'm saying,' Klugg said with a nod. 'But I want a gentleman's agreement. If you get me, then I want to be buried on that little hill just outside of town. If I get you, I want to be free to take my money and ride out of here.'

Keeping his eyes on Klugg, Vejar called to the sheriff, 'Do you hear that, George?'

'I hear, Fallon. I'm out of this, anyway. The Malone girl is holding a gun on me.'

Old loyalties die hard, Vejar acknowledged, as he thought of Gloria. Then the situation he was in suddenly hit Vejar hard. This was a long way from being the first time he had faced a man in a shoot-out, but Klugg's speed on the draw meant there was nothing between them. Vejar was vividly aware that within minutes one of them would die.

Klugg made his move, lightning fast. Vejar drew, certain that he had shaded the outlaw leader, but a bullet hit him, the impact knocking

158

him off balance. Staying on his feet, Vejar realized that he had been hit in the left shoulder. There was no pain yet, but when he put his hand to the shoulder it came away covered in blood. Bracing himself for Klugg's finishing shot, he turned, determined to be facing the man who killed him. But Klugg lay dead in the dust. A small stain on the front of the outlaw leader's shirt made it evident that Vejar's bullet had found his heart. Clutching his shoulder as pain kicked in, Vejar walked to the teashop, feet dragging.

Early the following morning, Sheriff Harker made his way towards the Alcotts' home. There was a slight break in the rhythm of his walk as he came closer to the house. It was as though the sheriff had lost confidence in himself. Yesterday had ended better than anyone could have wished. Randall's nephew was already on the mend, and the bank raid had failed. But the death of young Len had marred the day. His own injuries all but forgotten, he had locked up Gloria Malone in the jail while Doc Thurston had attended Vejar's shoulder wound. That wound had been serious enough for the doctor to insist that Vejar remain in the Chua place for the night.

Herbert Alcott opened the door to Harker, inviting him in. He found Raya in the kitchen cooking breakfast. Turning to greet him with a smile, her face paled and her expression changed when she saw the look on his face.

'What is it, George?' she enquired, her voice shaky.

Harker beckoned to have her walk out to the front door with him, not wanting any of the Alcott family see Raya's reaction to his reply. He told her, 'Fallon had gone when I got up this morning.'

'Oh,' Raya said unhappily. Then she brightened. 'I've heard that he killed the Poole brothers. He probably wanted to get away because of that.'

'That was self-defence. Fallon wouldn't have faced any charges,' Harker explained. 'There is something else, Raya. I found Gloria Malone's cell unlocked this morning, and she had gone. Fallon had a key to the jail.'

Raya bit her bottom lip and fought back tears as understanding dawned on her. She looked to where the worn trail out of Yancey meandered off to the foothills. She wondered wistfully, 'Do you think that we'll ever see either of them again, George?'

'Maybe not. But they are two of a kind, Raya, and I'm sure we'll often hear about them,' Harker said, tentatively placing an arm round her shoulders. He waited anxiously, then tightened his arm as Raya cuddled against him.